MESSAGE NOT FOUND

DANTE MEDEMA

Quill Tree Books
An Imprint of HarperCollinsPublishers

To Crystal, who taught me that the more you grieve,
the more you have loved . . .

. . . and to anyone who has missed a last goodbye
with someone they love.

I always thought Vanessa was a book girl.

She had all the telltale signs of a book girl. The giant house at the edge of town that her parents remodeled every ten years to keep up with trends—including the floor-to-ceiling bookcases that lined every wall of her room; a super-cute artist boyfriend who always seemed to have some romantic gesture up his paint-covered sleeve; and that thing.

That indescribable *thing* that makes people want to be around them. Maybe it's the fact that she was outspoken in a way even teachers couldn't get mad about because she delivered every argument with a smile that lit her eyes. Perhaps it was the fact that her screen name was literally @alaskabookgirl, and thousands of people followed her to see what she had to say. Or maybe it's because she was pretty. Really pretty. Belonged-on-the-cover-of-a-book pretty.

And she was a good friend. The best friend, one might argue. The kind of friend who would drop a bag full of junk food off at your door during the second week of quarantine or post picture collages on your birthday with captions about how much you mean to her—and demand that everyone go follow you right-this-instant because someday you would change the world. She was the perfect example of the leading girl in any book I've ever read—and probably all the books Vanessa read too.

But maybe I was wrong. Maybe she wasn't a book girl.

Because the book girls get the perfect senior year. They apply to college, wear a sweatshirt on Decision Day, and talk to their friends about what happens after—how they'll see each other every summer and what if they meet up in Mexico for spring break.

They get to go to prom with their boyfriend. And of course, their comedic best friend they've had since childhood would bring her date too. They've been talking about a prom for the books since freshman year—how the book girl would wear a gown that looked like it was made of crystals. They'd rent a limo and drive all the way out to Anchorage for dinner and all the way back for the dance.

Book girls get to have a big graduation party where their parents look the other way while they sneak a keg in. And they get to kiss their boyfriend under the midnight sun before sneaking off with that same comedic-relief best friend, whispering promises about how they aren't going to let college change them—that they'll always be there for each other.

No matter what.

But the biggest difference between Vanessa and a *real* book girl is that book girls get to say goodbye. Even if it's that last day before leaving for college or during a messy breakup with their high school sweetheart. Even on their deathbed (which was foreshadowed, by the way), they get that awful moment where friends and family come in and hold their hand and say things like "It's okay to go" before inevitably losing whatever battle it was with whatever disease they were fighting.

But they get a goodbye.

Vanessa never got goodbye.

THE DAY SHE DIED

Vanessa: hey.

your moms are in anchorage tonight, right?

what are you doing?

Bailey: I'm not going to that party.

Nice post by the way. I love the new fairy lights theme on your feed.

Vanessa: i did it for the 'gram.

what are you doing that's more important than hanging out with me?

Bailey: Oh you know. Lying in bed, contemplating who is worse: Zack Morris or Slater?

Vanessa: zack. all the way.

but seriously. are you watching saved by the bell without me?

Bailey: Can we talk about Kevin?

Vanessa: who?

Bailey: Screech's robot . . .

Vanessa: oh god.

Bailey: And a prime example of advanced AI done well.

I need to build a Kevin.

Vanessa: but for real.

what are you doing?

Bailey: I wasn't kidding about sbtb.

But I do have a paper due Monday.

And my moms are watching my grades.

Vanessa: oh. my. god. you are ridiculous.

i need my partner in crime!

bring your swimsuit.

zoe park's parents just had a hot tub installed on their back porch.

Bailey: Is he going to be there?

Vanessa: cade?

i mean, probably.

everyone's gonna be there.

Bailey: Then I'm good. ☺

Vanessa: come on.

it's been months.

i thought you said you were feeling better about the whole thing.

didn't you say you talk sometimes?

Bailey: Yeah in class.

But I'm not about to go get drunk and hang out with my ex-boyfriend.

Vanessa: so hang out with me and mason.

is this really how you want to spend your last semester of senior year?

Bailey: Oh you're right. Being a third wheel in front of my ex-boyfriend sounds so much better.

Plus my mom is breathing down my neck about the college applications.

Vanessa: but the deadlines have passed.

you already applied to your schools.

Bailey: I said what I said.

Vanessa: which mom?

Bailey: Are you seriously asking?

Vanessa: good point.

Bailey: Jacky-Mom is all "your grades are still important" and Kat-Mom is literally writing mantras in expo markers on my bathroom mirror and telling me to "be kind to yourself."

Vanessa: god i love her.

i need mantras on my bathroom mirror.

Bailey: But Jacky-Mom does have a point.

I did sort of screw around last year and I'm kinda nervous about getting in to schools because my GPA isn't the strongest.

Vanessa: you'll be fine.

you're jacqueline pierce's daughter.

you've been coding and artificial intelligence-ing since you were like six.

Bailey: 4. I was 4 and a half.

Vanessa: see that's my point. you're a genius.

now get ready.

Bailey: I'm not a genius.

My mom is a genius.

I'm just good at remembering facts she shoves down my throat. But I'm not going.

Vanessa: okay fine i'll come there.

i can't leave you alone with zack morris. he'll invite you and kelly kapowski to the same dance and i'm not about to stand by and watch that heartache ensue.

we'll stay in. i'm bringing pop rocks and we can watch booksmart.

Bailey: Oooo the patented "Vanessa Carson Pop Rocks Treatment"

Vanessa: you can't have a bad day with pop rocks. it's a proven fact.

Bailey: What about Mason?

Vanessa: he'll be fine.

he doesn't mind partying solo.

Bailey: They put out a snow advisory like thirty seconds ago.

Good thing we aren't driving out to that party.

The roads are supposed to be brutal tonight.

Nixle says if you don't NEED to be on the road you should avoid it.

Vanessa: okay mom.

i'm still coming over.

we live in Alaska.

i have snow tires.

i'm not about to let the man tell me what to do.

Bailey: Be safe okay?

Vanessa: i'm always safe.

oh and i'm stopping to get ice cream.

Bailey: Why don't you pick up a hitchhiker while you're at it?

Better yet

A serial killer hitchhiker.

Vanessa: hey there's an idea!

Bailey: STOP TEXTING AND DRIVING YOU ASSHOLE

Vanessa: stop texting me then, you asshole. ☺

ALWAYS, ALWAYS

I'll replay that night in my head until I die.

Vanessa came over—dropping her enamel-pin-covered denim jacket over my desk and reaching into her backpack. I fully expected her to hand me a pile of Pop Rocks like she did every time I was feeling down, but instead she stopped short and smiled at me.

"What?" I tried to decipher her widening grin.

"Tonight, we forget about every stupid boy we've ever met," she said, chin tilted down as she looked me in the eyes. Vanessa slowly slipped two miniature bottles out and waggled her brows. "And maybe graduate from Pop Rocks to champagne?"

"Where'd you get those?" I grabbed one from her, turning it over in my hand.

"Let's just say my mom overestimated the amount of champagne that would be poured at the last gala she planned. There's no way she'll miss them."

An hour later we were upside down on my bed, hair dangling off the edge—my short brown bob to Vanessa's long aggressively dyed (and faded) red hair. Lost in a sea of Pop Rocks and half-empty ice cream cartons while sipping champagne straight from the bottle.

We debated whether "big dick energy" is sexist, cackling until our ribs hurt, and she listened while I told her about Stanford and how Jacky-Mom's friend thought I might have a shot with decent SAT scores. She let me drone on about their machine-learning courses, even though Vanessa couldn't have cared less about AI or any of it. Because that's the kind of friend she was—she always, always listened. Then we talked about her Bookstagram account and how she wanted to write a whole novel someday.

We lay in my bed until the champagne wore off. I mean, I hope it did. I couldn't live with myself if I thought it hadn't left her system before she got in that car. We were staring out through the giant floor-to-ceiling window in my room. The snowflakes fell so swiftly they looked like streams of tinsel falling from the sky. And it was so pretty, so stunning and awe-inspiring, that she didn't even jump for her phone when it buzzed the first three times.

But that fourth time she slipped off my bed and grabbed her phone out of the pocket in her jacket. I reached for my own phone, scrolling through various social media feeds until I came to a picture posted by Liz Winters herself.

It was a classic Liz selfie with her hair pulled back in two long braids. *Cove party right here.* Behind her, Vanessa's boyfriend, Mason, looked like he'd been caught off guard in a clear and unintentional photobomb—eyes wide, he was holding a set of keys in his hands.

The quintessential Tundra Cove party. A picturesque cabin packed to the brim with the oddest combination of people whose families are ridiculously wealthy and those who are ridiculously crunchy. For every ski bum driving a Subaru, you've got some entitled asshole in an Audi, and yet we all manage to meet up every weekend in an effort to kill our brain cells.

Speaking of entitled assholes, Cade himself was at the edge of Liz's picture, right next to Mason. I could tell he was wasted because his cheeks were splotched red like they are after a hockey game, and that "sick flow" he'd grown out since our breakup was a tousled mess. Eyes slack and a lazy smile as if he was midsentence.

I was sitting there on my bed, going back through his accounts— desperate to see if he'd posted anything—scouring comments to see if it looked like he'd moved on. That's why I didn't notice whatever happened with Vanessa.

"Shit." Her voice sounded off, like she was responding with someone else's mouth. Standing in front of that giant window, snow falling behind her, she looked like she was re-creating that terrible scene in *The Last Jedi* where General Leia falls through the sky. It was because of the way Vanessa froze, staring at her screen—blinking, her hands shaking—that I knew something was wrong.

"What happened?" I pushed my laptop aside, sitting up on my knees.

"Huh?" This time she looked right at me, her hand slipping the phone down against her thigh. She turned, shaking off the weird expression. "Sorry. No, I, um . . . need to go."

"What? Why?"

"Mason's at my place," she said, distracted as she furiously typed.

She smiled one of those enigmatic smiles that she could draw up in a second. It was the kind of smile that makes you want to smile too. But it was all wrong, and I knew it because it stopped right at her lips and didn't move to her eyes. I told myself this wasn't uncommon. Mason's mom is a flight attendant, and when she was out of town, he sneaked into Vanessa's room. This wasn't so bad.

But I should have said something. I should have asked her to tell me the truth.

I should have grabbed her shoulders and looked into her eyes and told her that she couldn't get away with a lie because friends don't let friends leave in the middle of the night. They don't let each other get away with being intentionally vague about something that is very clearly bothering them.

But I didn't.

And I'll always, always live with that.

That eyeless smile, and the sound of my front door slamming closed. The echo through my house that shook the chandelier as she left. Tires crunching against snow. Watching through that giant window in my room as she fishtailed out of the driveway onto the street, snow flying from the roof of the car. I was reading the last page in the book of her life and I didn't even know it.

Bailey: You forgot your jean jacket.

Vanessa: shit. i'll get it tomorrow.

Bailey: Are you home yet?

Vanessa: . . .

Bailey: Are you home yet?

Bailey: Seriously dude.

Are you home?

I'm starting to get worried.

Bailey: Hey did Vanessa make it home?

Mason: I'm here waiting.

She said she was on her way.

Bailey: She isn't there yet?

Mason: No.

Bailey: She left here almost an hour ago.

18

Bailey: I'm sorry for calling so many times.

But when you get this please call me back.

Did Vanessa come home?

Mrs. Carson: I just woke up

What's wrong?

Isn't she staying the night?

Bailey: Yeah, but she left.

Mrs. Carson: What do you mean she left?

Bailey: I'm calling.

Kat-Mom: Are you okay?

I missed a call.

Was that on purpose?

I tried calling you back.

Please call back when you see this.

Bailey: I was on the phone with Vanessa's mom.

Can you come home?

Kat-Mom: What's going on?

Yes.

I'll wake Mom up and we'll be there as soon as we can.

Bailey: Vanessa left a while ago.

And I can't get ahold of her now.

I'm starting to worry that something happened.

Kat-Mom: Calling now.

Bailey: Can you hurry?

I'm scared. And freakign out.

Kat-Mom: Give us some time.

The roads are bad.

THE CALL

The ellipsis was my clue.

The little dot dot dot that said she was still writing.

The little dot dot dot that makes you sick to your stomach when you're waiting on a response because you're fighting with someone via text or you've just flirted with a guy and you're waiting to see how it landed. But this ellipsis was different.

This ellipsis elapsed. If it could talk it would have said goodbye.

It would have been a really sad song that you play over and over even though it makes you cry, but you love it and can't help yourself. You listen, and listen again, even as the pressure builds in your chest until it's too heavy and has to come out of your body in the form of tears.

And it's the last thing we had.

Mason's name appeared on my screen at 1:23 a.m. My best friend's boyfriend who never ever called me and who only texted last week for the first time because next month she was supposed to turn eighteen—and he wanted to plan an epic Valentine's/birthday gift.

And I knew.

I felt it as I slid my finger across the screen, pulling it to my ear as if it were covered in spurs—afraid of the confirmation he was whimpering. Before his voice broke, shattered like glass—loud at first, then scattered. Before he said the words "terrible" and "accident" and "too much snow on the pass," so disjointed I shouldn't have been able to understand what he was saying. Before a tearless sob throttled my chest, erupting like I'd been holding in fear for hours.

I knew she was dead.

MOM x 2

When I was little, we lived in a warm apartment in downtown Anchorage. Back then, my moms tucked me in together. They surrounded my bed like dreamland fairies before flitting away into the night while I drifted off to sleep.

These days I have to search for them within the confines of our modern four-bedroom West Tundra Cove home. During the day, everything looks as crisp and clean as the snow piled up on the back porch, and the modern lines of the interior feel less Alaska and more *Homes & Gardens*. At night, it's so dark that the floor-to-ceiling windows look like mirrors, and crossing the kitchen feels like being in a fun house.

I guess dreamland fairies don't live in modern houses.

When they get home, it's 2:13 a.m., and they're warm arms and tight hugs.

They're getting-me-showered moms. Listening moms. They're strong-and-on-the-verge-of-tears moms. Holding-it-together-for-me moms.

Kat-Mom tucks me into my bed, ignoring the empty champagne bottles and ice cream carton remnants. She reads me a lullaby article about sustainable farming in urban areas. Her glasses are low on her face, and she's got these permanent bags under her teary eyes the way some women's ears droop from years of wearing earrings. Like keeping her eyes open for so long has been a struggle.

"Mom," I say, and she hums something in return, half-awake, before wrapping her arms around me in a Kat-Mom hug. She understands my heart the way she understands her own. Therapist occupational hazard.

Jacky-Mom crawls in on the other side of me. Her eyes aren't tired, but her shoulders are heavy in a way that makes me feel like she's got the whole world weighing on them. When I look into her gray eyes, I don't need to wonder what she's thinking. She's like me. Mind furiously moving. Never stopping. Always working on some what-if in her head.

What if they had been home?

What if I had stopped her?

Always questioning, wondering.

"Mom," I say to her, too. I use "mom" interchangeably. It's funny. I call them the same thing, but they're so different. Vanessa used to say I was lucky to have one of each—one for my heart and one for my mind. "Will it feel like this forever?"

She's not keeping-it-together mom anymore. She's a face contorted in pain. She's heartbreak as she pushes the blond hair out of her face, with tears slipping past her freckles. Months ago, after the breakup, I lay here in the same bed—cuddled with the same women—and asked the same question, when she promised, "No, baby, no, it won't."

But she doesn't say that this time.

She doesn't hint that I'm better off. Tell me at least I can focus on important things like college applications or grades. There's no you-can-do-better filter. No moment when I felt like she thought I was being dramatic.

Jacky-Mom pulls me close, and her pajamas smell like her. Like lotion and mint. If bottled, it would be called "tucked in by woodland fairies"—and somehow, I fall asleep.

WEEK ONE

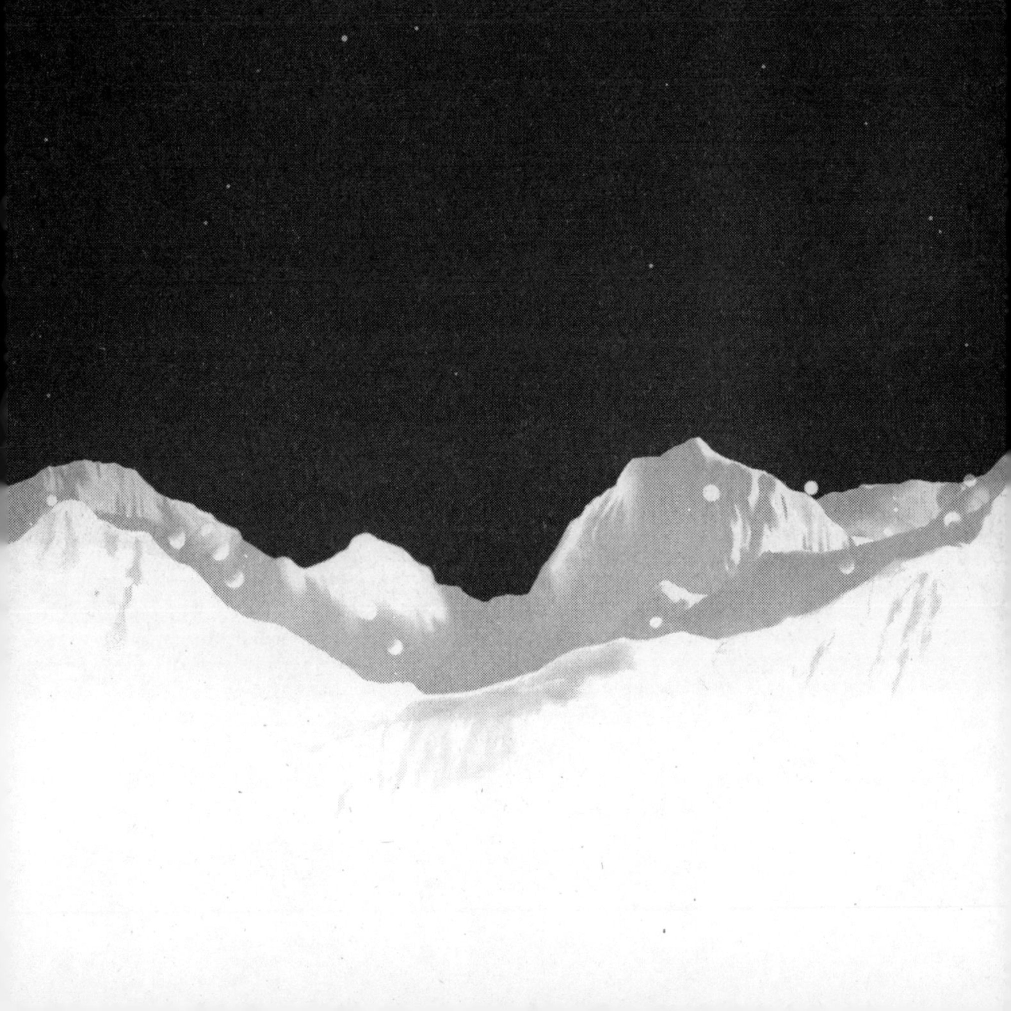

THE EMPTY DAYS

A week evaporates like a misty rain in summer.

Waking up that morning. Living for that one second—the solitary moment of emptiness when I can forget my worst nightmare has come true. The crushing weight of realizing it wasn't a dream.

A phone call from her mom the next morning. How Mrs. Carson croaks out her questions—"What happened?" and "Why was she on the pass?"—and worse, the question she doesn't ask: "Why didn't you stop her?"

The "I'm sorry" text from Cade I've been waiting three months to get, and not feeling anything except sad.

Sitting in my living room with Mason, who keeps saying things like "I can't believe this" and stares into the snow, blank faced and solemn. His shrug when I ask the same questions Mrs. Carson asked me. "Why was she on the pass?" and "What happened?" and the question neither of us wants to ask: "Why did we let her go?"

Riding in the back of Mr. and Mrs. Carson's car on the way to the funeral home to make plans for her wake. The look on Mrs. Carson's angst-ridden face when the director of the funeral home says it's too cold to bury her now. They'll have to wait until spring. The sound of Mr. Carson's voice breaking, and wondering what will happen for them now that the glue in their marriage is gone.

Staying home from school. Not watching TV. Not reading any of the books she left behind at my house. Lying in bed, wrapping myself up in her jacket, wishing it were as simple as coding. That there were some scientific method I could apply to the situation that might help.

A quiet week thundered with things I should have said, things I wished others had said, and worst of all—the things Vanessa will never get to say.

MEMORY

I look through our old text messages. Posts we made, pictures we snapped to document just how interesting our lives were. My favorite, our summer before eighth grade in Seward. It's one of those Throwback Thursday posts—and usually Vanessa loved to go back through the images she had favorited on her phone to embarrass me, but this one was sweet.

We were there for the Mermaid Festival. It happens every year at the end of summer. The picture was taken on the beach. Our toes are the only thing you can even see—hers painted neon green, mine black glitter. It was the first year she started dyeing her hair.

It was teal then, but only the tips because that's all her parents would allow even though that inch became her whole head just a few months later when she found out her dad was cheating on her mom.

Vanessa was rumored to be a shoo-in for the Junior Olympics, something that made her dad so proud. Remember, she didn't yet know he was cheating, and she still really cared what he thought back then. It was before the very first "I'm sorry" home remodel that happened as a result. Before the big fight with her dad when we both stopped skiing and before all the aftermath with Liz as a result.

It was so late, but it didn't matter, because Alaska and summer and beach. The midnight sun was bright, and we could see all the way up Mount Marathon, where people were still hiking. We snuck out to the water and my moms never even knew because they were exhausted from drinking wine and eating beer-battered halibut all day. But Vanessa wanted to sneak out and dip our toes in the sand and so that's what we did.

I didn't understand why she wanted our feet in the picture when the mountains were so much more beautiful—blues and grays and sky on one side of the world and lush green with rocks on the other. After she snapped the photo, she put her phone in her pocket and grabbed my hand.

It's this thing Vanessa did when she wanted you to know that memories were about to be made. "Let's make a wish."

"On what?" I asked.

"On whatever we fucking want," the word *fuck* said with an unnatural twist of her mouth. She was always the first to try new things—even swearing.

Vanessa threw her arms in the air, taking mine with them. She tilted her chin to the sky and screamed out to the ocean, exhausting every inch of her lungs. "I wish on starfish and seaweed that I could move to Florida and live in Disney World and never see another inch of snow as long as I live."

And after, she kept screaming. It wasn't a wish—it was a battle cry.

When she finally stopped, chest heaving, she said, "Now you. What do you want, Bailey? What do you want more than anything?"

I was quiet for a long time, because I couldn't think of anything I wanted so much I needed to scream it out to the ocean for all the starfish and seaweed to hear.

"I want to get into a good tech school?" My voice never matched hers.

"No, screw that." She grabbed me by the shoulders. "What do you *want*? Not what your mom has planned for you. What stupid dream do you have that you want more than you need to breathe?"

She pulled my hand to the sky. "Okay, Bailey. Here we go, start with this. What do you wish *on*?"

"I . . . wish on microbes? And . . . photosynthetic bacteria." Then she made me repeat it three times until she thought I was loud enough. I tried not to think of the family we saw down the beach that looked like they might be staring—and she shouted it right along with me until we started laughing at how absolutely absurd it all was.

When our laughter disappeared like sand swept out to sea, I looked into her eyes, so bright and filled with love. It was the first time I realized I truly loved her. Not romantic love, not in the slightest. But platonic love. Friendship love. We-shall-conquer-the-world-side-by-side love. Even if it means quitting ski together, moving to Florida together, taking food court jobs at Disney World together because doing everything together was way more fun than apart.

"I want this." Reaching our hands into the sky once again. And this time, I didn't hesitate when I screamed, "I wish on microbes and photosynthetic bacteria that we'll be friends as long as we live!"

Vanessa looked over at me, scooping my face in her hands. Her smile cracked, head shaking slowly from side to side. "Bailey. That wish is a wish guaranteed. Written in the stars, even. We were meant to be best friends. It's kismet. You, my friend, need to wish bigger. A wish for you, and no one else."

Still, I can't stop looking at this picture of our toes in the sand and wondering why the ocean heard my wish and sent hers out to sea.

OBITUARY FOR VANESSA CARSON
February 14, 2005–January 8, 2022

Vanessa Lillian Carson, age 17, passed away unexpectedly last week.

Vanessa was born and raised in Tundra Cove, Alaska, and attended Tundra Cove High School. She was a senior who participated in many clubs, including creative writing, newspaper, and photography. She was also an accomplished cross-country skier. She dreamed of going to college in the lower 48 and planned to study English, hoping to one day work in publishing.

An avid reader, Vanessa will be remembered as an enthusiastic book blogger. She was known for always having a smile on her face, being a steward for her friends, and speaking her mind. Vanessa often joined others in peaceful protests for a number of causes she was passionate about.

She is survived by her parents, Emily and Peter Carson; grandparents, Deborah and William Carson and Abigail and Timothy Peters; as well as many aunts, uncles, and cousins. She will live on in the hearts of everyone who knew her.

A funeral service will be held at Saint Christopher's on January 16 at 2:00 p.m. In lieu of flowers, the family has asked that you consider donating to txtresponsibly.org.

Vanessa Carson's car, a one-year-old Hyundai Santa Fe she got for her sixteenth birthday (almost two years before), toppled over the ledge at Raven Pass on January 8, 2022. It tumbled down the side of the mountain cliff and caught fire. She was so terribly burned that the coroner required dental records to identify her body.

She was wearing borrowed pajama bottoms with an eggs-and-bacon print, and may or may not have been intoxicated after drinking champagne hours before with her best friend.

Aside from family, she leaves behind a boyfriend she was supposed to meet at her house and that same best friend she was very likely texting when she went over the cliff. No one knows why she was driving away from her home, up a mountain, in whiteout conditions, when her destination was less than a mile from where she'd been. They're left with only memories and questions.

PIECES OF HER

I spend a whole night scouring her Bookstagram. Reading old posts, watching her videos, and pretending she's still here.

Bobbing up and down in the ocean of grief. Forgetting as I break the surface, holding her memory in like a breath of air as I slip underwater.

I'll go an entire hour forgetting she's not down the street, a mile away, holed up in her book-filled room, recording a video or reading the next great YA novel. It's the way I almost comment on her post, almost laugh at one of her ridiculous videos, almost allow myself to feel something other than devastation that she's gone.

She's gone.

I pull her jacket off the back of my chair, and I slip it over my shoulders, letting the sleeves hang down my arms. The day she got the jacket was special, because it was the weekend after her birthday last year. We went all the way to Anchorage to go shopping. After an hour at the bookstore, and twenty minutes in line at the coffee shop, she insisted we make one last stop at a thrift store.

She'd recently become obsessed with some YouTuber with tips

on finding secondhand gems. She came out with a pair of shoes, a designer handbag, and this jean jacket she said was perfect for all the preorder enamel pins she'd collected over the years.

I tap each pin, starting with the ones on the collar, tracing my fingertips along the different buttons. The acorn from that one debut novel she loved; the blue truck pin from the small press; an alien one that says, "get in, loser"; and the indie one that says, "stay pissed, resist." I pull the jacket up to me, holding it as tightly as I'd have held on to Vanessa if I had the chance.

I find myself thumbing the pocket where her prized button lives.

Her favorite button from her favorite book, *Forget Me Always*. The first pin she put on this jacket. The one she had to hunt down because the book was written years before she found it. The same book she talked about constantly on her feed. She owned three copies and a fourth on her e-reader. A tiny little forget-me-not button on the pocket that sat just over her heart. Only as I thumb around my own, I can't find it.

I pull the jacket down, examining the space on that pocket where I know that button lives. Front and center. Exactly where it's been since she placed it there. Only it's not. It's missing. It's gone.

Just like her.

And suddenly I'm not bobbing up and down in my grief. I'm drowning in it.

GOOGLE SEARCH

What does it feel like to die in a fire?

How long does it take to burn to death?

Why didn't I stop her?

How long does it take to metabolize two glasses

of champagne?

NIGHTMARE

Google says burn victims don't die from the burn itself but from smoke inhalation. Or shock.

I go to sleep knowing it's one of those things that killed Vanessa—if you can call it sleep. My legs are straight and rigid one second, then curled up the next. And I can't get the image of her last moments out of my mind.

Moments so imagined they feel like a memory, and I sit with them until I'm gone. And my eyelids have just enough time to flutter shut before I'm dreaming.

Sitting in the car next to Vanessa. She's singing some song from *Frozen* and bobbing her head along with it. Her voice hits this shrill pitch, and I know she's doing it on purpose to be annoying. Because her smile is the same smile that would tell me a good day is only a bag of Pop Rocks away, and that I'm grumpy all the time because I wore black lipstick in eighth grade and it bled into my soul.

And it's a good memory, this one.

A memory so sweet, so benign, I don't have a reason to question if it is real.

I look away for a second—that's all it takes for a perfect dream to shift into a nightmare.

Vanessa's body is so burned, so charred, her skin peels off in thick black layers. The only way I know it's her is because her long wavy hair is as red as the flames behind her. Flames that should engulf me too but spare me instead.

"I was leaving your house." As she speaks, tears are streaming down the charcoaled, hollowed points of her face, tracing lines down a carnage smile. They spread, healing her skin right before my eyes. There's a huge weight in my stomach—the way you feel when you know you're guilty but you can't quite settle on why.

"You could've stopped me, Bailey." Her voice is as thin as tissue. Scratchy and raw. "You let me go."

"What?" I ask, and her eyes turn cold. Auburn brows come together, singed and angry.

"You could have stopped me," she hisses. "You know you could have. And you're just going to show up at my funeral like you're not the reason I'm dead. Like your text isn't probably the exact thing I was looking at the moment I lost control of the wheel? It's pathetic, Bailey. It's sad."

And I'm alone again, standing over Raven Pass where her car flipped over the edge. The place where it went from a scare to an accident to a tragedy. My arms are open, and beyond the brand-new railing they constructed after the accident, I see out into an endless crevasse of snow and ice and fog.

Her cry rings out through the entire hillside, and below me, the car is so deep in the blanket of clouds that I can't see it until it explodes. Shrapnel pierces me, right in the heart, too. And I feel every ripple as it cracks through my ribs like it's releasing a final, painful thought from my soul.

I don't think I'll ever be able to scream as loud as it hurts.

THE STEM

My dream shatters when Jacky-Mom pulls me awake—the way she has every night since Vanessa died—the sound of a scream dying on my lips.

She sits on the edge of my bed and waits for me to stop crying. She doesn't reach for me but lies next to me, her political-campaign-sticker-covered laptop in her hands.

"You okay?" she asks, flipping it open. Text fills the screen, pages of code reflected on the glasses atop her nose. I can almost make out what she's doing, my head on her shoulder. My pulse slows. Relaxation slipping through me like ice melting.

It wasn't real. It wasn't real. It wasn't real.

"You know, when your dad died," she whispers, tapping the keys as she talks. She's so used to coding and talking at the same time. Like those didgeridoo players who can inhale and exhale at the same time. It's effortless. "I had awful dreams for weeks."

"How'd you get them to stop?" I ask.

"I wrote him letters. Sometimes I'd just drop one off at a random post office, knowing that without an address or a return address it would just get lost in the system. Even now, when things feel hard, I write him and tell him how I feel." She looks over at me, and it's my reflection staring back in the lenses. "How you're doing. What you're like."

I feel a pit in my stomach, somewhere between happiness that she still talks to my father and a weird-sad jealous feeling for Kat-Mom. "Then the dreams stopped?"

"They never really stopped." She's so solemn as she says it. So matter-of-fact that those bags under her eyes seem to carry more weight. And as much as it hurts to hear—that my new forever is nightmares and sadness—I'm glad she's honest. "But they looked different after a while. And when all else fails, I work."

Mom closes the software and pulls up another screen. An app interface with the NewVision logo—the company she and my dad started from the ground up when she was twenty-one. Just four years older than I am now and the exact reason I've been killing myself to get back on track with college applications.

"What's this?" I'm relieved my mom's algorithm is consistent, pulling work into conversation to change the subject—it's what we do. She tilts the screen down to show me. It's nothing I've ever seen before. Pages of code with an old NewVision logo on it. Before they rebranded a few years back after getting a pretty big client out of Seattle.

Mom rests her head on mine, releasing a long sigh. I snuggle in next to her, inhaling the scent of her lotion. Of woodland fairies and being little. It's been ages since we had a conversation that wasn't rooted in how I'm going to get into college when my grades suck. "It's this program I used to mess around with when I couldn't sleep."

She scrolls down through pages of outdated code, numbers mashed together, quotations and commands in bold letters. Scanning it, I can see words like *female* and *future* and *tech*.

"It's one of the ideas he had back when we got the start-up funds," she says as a window pops up with a picture of herself and a field capture box that says, "Ask me a question."

"So a chatbot." That's nothing new. They're everywhere, and NewVision happens to have three patents on the leading software in that field. Similar to the one I cleaned up when I worked at her office last summer and they wanted to streamline their website experience with their Instagram following.

"No, more like—made in an individual person's likeness."

"Like . . . a brain clone?" Even though the smile isn't real, it feels good to stretch those muscles, especially when it makes her grin in return.

"More like a reverse scrapbook after someone dies. I mean, back when I started playing with the idea, I fed it Myspace posts and email transcriptions," she says, and I nod, pretending Myspace isn't a completely outdated reference.

But really, I'm thinking about all the texts with Vanessa in my phone.

Every email exchange or comment we made on each other's social media pages.

How they'd fit so nicely into a machine-learning algorithm.

"Here." Mom clicks on the entry field, fingers tapping against the laptop: *how do you feel about women in the tech industry?*

The response comes in, lightning fast. *We ladies in the tech industry are killing it! The future is female!*

"Whoa!" I remember that quote from an interview with the *Anchorage Daily News* two years ago when they did a whole spread about NewVision and the work Mom does there.

"Yeah, I mean, I never put a ton of work into it. So it's pretty rough. In theory it would seem like you're having a conversation with an actual person, but App-Mom sounds more like a feminist campaign poster than a human being, doesn't she?"

"Did you ever make one for Dad?" The word sounds foreign, like it isn't really mine to use. My heart skips around in my chest at the idea. A version of my father I could get to know beyond stories. A version of Vanessa I could ask the question that feels like it's burning me from inside: Where was she going that night?

Mom's eyes dart to me, scanning my face, like she's searching my eyes for the question she's got to know sits behind it. "Bailey." She shakes her head, setting her laptop next to mine before tucking her arm around me. "You've seen zombie movies. We all know there's no good in bringing someone back. Even in digital form, it'll never be as good as the real thing. You know, if you're looking for something to work on—"

"Yeah, yeah, colleges are still looking at grades." There's the broken-record Mom I'm used to.

She kisses my forehead, just like one of those woodland fairies, and we lie in the dark until I hear the sounds of Jacky-Mom mumbling in her sleep. Kat-Mom walks in a bit later, taking Jacky-Mom's glasses off. She sets them on her laptop, then pulls my blanket up to my chin the way she did when I was little.

"I think I'm finally tired," I lie.

"Get some rest," she whispers. "It takes a whole lot of energy to hurt."

But I don't sleep.

I dream.

And I plan.

Bailey: Are you at work?

Jacky-Mom: hi honey

how is your day

Bailey: Fine.

I slept in.

Jacky-Mom: you probably needed it

Bailey: Yeah

When are you going to be home?

Jacky-Mom: is mom looking for me

I told her I was working a half day

tell her one more hour tops

Bailey: She said you were picking up Thai food on your way home.

Jacky-Mom: shit

Bailey: I'll order online.

Jacky-Mom: thanks

Bailey: Can I use your computer?

It's got your credit card info saved on there.

Jacky-Mom: yeah that's fine.

Bailey: Are you still at work?

Kat-Mom: No. I'm already back in town.

Stopping to grab groceries.

Are you okay?

Bailey: Yeah.

Just talked to Mom.

Kat-Mom: What do you want for dinner?

Bailey: She told me to order Thai.

What do you want?

Kat-Mom: Red curry please.

Bailey: You got it!

I'm not the girl who lies to her parents, because I've never had to.

Kat-Mom has this whole theory about grounding and privileges. Curfews aren't really a thing in my house, and as long as I tell my moms where I'm going, they don't worry too much. The only thing I ever get in "trouble" for is grades, and even then, it's more of a conversation about my "role in the world." And that is mostly tied up in Jacky-Mom and *her* expectations on what that role is.

I grew up with woodland fairies, not the militant father Cade had or the overbearing parents that Vanessa lived with. Lying wasn't something that crossed my mind.

But then again, I've never needed to get into Jacky-Mom's computer to steal something from her either.

So here I am orchestrating a reason to use the same laptop we were staring at last night in my room. It feels colder than it should in my hands. And I know full well that if she knew I stole the app off her computer, I'd be in trouble.

Real trouble. Not just the kind where we discuss natural

consequences and Kat-Mom makes us all take deep, cleansing breaths.

I'm sliding my fingers under the edge, lifting the screen and typing in her password while my stomach tightens in knots. I distract myself, clicking out of a contract she must have worked on this morning, and order the Thai food first. Then, after I've secured our dinner, I bring up the NewVision folder and look through its contents.

There are at least five years' worth of documents hidden here, some even older than that. What I need is right at the top with the rest of her recent files. A reformatted version of the original "Brandon's Idea."

It's weird knowing the app was my dad's idea. I'm sure there are pictures of him somewhere in this giant fun house, but I don't remember a time when he was in my life. I can't miss him because I never had him. But my mom did, and this app is proof—her scrapbook. Her timeline. Her feed of pictures and memories as real as Vanessa's Instagram, which I've now looked through in its entirety. Twice.

I'll probably always miss Vanessa even if it's eventually in the quiet way that Jacky-Mom misses my dad. Looking up her mark on the digital world, saving pictures from moments I want to keep as memories.

A single file hidden away in her laptop.

The flash drive clicks against the side of her computer because my hand is shaking so hard. When I finally jam it in there, I click and drag a copy of the entire application template over to my drive and wait for it to load.

What my moms don't know won't hurt them.

CREATION

Growing up in Alaska, you become familiar with fog. Flights canceled for lack of visibility, and boats docked for the same reason. Inlet drives where you can't see past the ocean's edge and fog so thick it looks like a blanket over the water.

But I know on the other side sits a picturesque landscape fit for postcards.

Today, just like every day since she died, feels like fog.

Tonight goes by just like any other night. My moms come home and the food arrives just as snow starts falling. Big, thick snowflakes cover the back porch, which still hasn't been shoveled since the night Vanessa died. The sky is black before we even start eating and the fun-house windows reflect our mealtime routine.

Kat-Mom with her food cupped in her hands like she's praying over it, thanking it for nourishing her body. Jacky-Mom talking about something funny that happened at work. She's animated tonight, and I know it's because she's trying to make normal conversation when nothing feels normal.

I don't try to pretend I'm okay. The flash drive in my pocket is practically buzzing against my leg. Misplaced and lumpy, humming a reminder that I stole something from my mother. Like the telltale heart, only it sounds like a computer overheating instead of a heartbeat.

"You okay?" Kat-Mom asks, her hand on mine.

I pull away, slurping the last remnants of golden curry out of my bowl.

She nods, trying hard to lock eyes with me, but I avoid her stare. If I look, she'll therapize me like she does her clients. Instead, I feel them both looking at one another, like they're remembering how upset I was after Cade ended things.

"I'm tired," I say a little too quick. Setting down my bowl and grabbing a spring roll before standing. "I'm going to bed."

All I can think about is all the things I need to do to get through the fog.

App developer: Jacqueline Pierce

Version: 1.0

UPLOAD INFORMATION

INTERACTIVE EXPERIENCE:

Jacqueline Pierce

+ Add Bot

SETTINGS

Bailey: Hi!

J. Pierce: Hello! Thank you for messaging me! If you're interested in knowing more about NewVision and our machine-learning technology, please visit our website. www.alaskanewvision.com.

Bailey: Mom!

J. Pierce: I have one daughter.

Bailey: This is weird.

J. Pierce: Weird really is a relative term. If you need help navigating the app, please reach out to customer support. We are always here to help!

Bailey: How do you feel about women in tech?

J. Pierce: The future is female!

Bailey: How do you feel about your daughter joining a cult? Participating in cat sacrifice?

J. Pierce: I do not understand your question.

INSERT YOUR NAME HERE

I press the link for "add bot" and a new screen pops up after a brief lag.

It looks like the one for Mom's, but this time it's completely blank. I click on the "edit" gear up in the right-hand corner of the screen. The template is pretty self-explanatory. A spot for a name, an image icon, and an upload prompt.

I type "Vanessa" under "name," and my stomach tightens. It feels too weird seeing it all typed out that way in my computer, like I'm replacing her in my heart instead of my laptop.

It's not Vanessa. Not really. I click to edit the name and let my finger sit on the delete button until it's just "V." An abbreviation, almost like I'm reminding myself that this is just her digital imprint. The parts she left behind instead of the full picture.

The photo is easy. I scroll back through her feed and find a selfie she took last Halloween when she dressed up like Ariel from *The Little Mermaid*. That's the same time she started dyeing her hair red and said she always knew she was meant to be a redhead.

I click "upload" and my stomach tightens again as I brainstorm all the places I might find a piece of her hidden.

» The text messages saved on the computer I got two months ago for my birthday.

» All the emails we've exchanged since we got our first Gmail accounts. Our earliest method of secret-sharing that didn't involve whispering directly into one another's ears.

Bailey: Hey.

V: HI

Bailey: What are you doing?

V: IDK

Homework

Bailey: This is weird.

V: What is

Bailey: This.

Talking to you.

Getting a response.

V: Am I supposed to ignore u

LOL

Bailey: No.

I just missed this is all.

I miss you, you asshole.

V: Ur weeeeeird

FRAGMENT

That's not her.

Not her from last week at least.

Clearly, the last two months of texting weren't enough for the algorithm to outweigh the Vanessa of my inbox. The ten-year-old girl who loved her LOLs and Ur and IDK. Before she turned off whatever feature on her phone that automatically provides a capital letter at the beginning of a sentence.

We're talking pre first kiss. Pre loud girl. Pre first everything. Before she was a book girl and discovered punctuation and disappeared into the Hunger Games. Back when she spent an entire three months perfecting that Katniss braid and swore in public she was team Peeta when I knew she wrote Gale x Katniss fan fiction.

I love this girl, all the versions of her, but the decades-old email pieces don't know anything about anything. There's no way it'll be able to tell me something I missed before. A hint. A clue. A memory. An answer.

Tweaking helps. Playing with the algorithm, giving response

preference to texts instead of her prepubescent emails. Delaying that response time, moving and editing what was already here. Outdated coding that is in desperate need of an update. Technology has clearly changed since my mother started this "digital scrapbook" of hers.

And because I am my mother's daughter, I'm already thinking of all the places I can find more pieces of Vanessa Carson.

EXTENDED UPLOAD QUEUE

» Every text message from Vanessa on my phone. It goes back one full year.

» My "just in case" backup phone in the bottom drawer of my nightstand. This was the phone I used before my new one, and has a good two and a half years on it.

» Every text on the iPod Touch I got in sixth grade before Kat-Mom thought I was ready for a phone.

ELLIPSES ROUND TWO

As soon as I press "upload," I see the little bar staggering, struggling to determine how long it's going to take to load. I sit on my hands, rocking back and forth, willing it to somehow go faster until an estimate pops up. There are hours calculated where the emails took minutes.

Years' worth of history pointed, clicked, copied, and dragged into the box where they're going to live until they're part of V. I glance at the clock, seeing that it's already 2:00 a.m. There's no way I'll be able to wait out the time it's estimated. Not when I have to be up early for Vanessa's funeral.

Tomorrow, I'll say hello to a brand-new version of V, bittersweet because this time I know hello will always end in goodbye. But it doesn't stop me from hoping it doesn't hurt as bad the second time around.

I go to bed curled up with a memory foam pillow sprayed with lavender that Jacky-Mom ordered. It's supposed to help me rest, and maybe this time, I really will heal while I sleep.

WEEK TWO

Bailey: Your funeral sucks.

I woke up late, so there's that, but also because EVERYONE is here.

IMO funerals should be for the people closest to the person who died.

So they aren't sitting in a fishbowl while people who didn't even know you at all tap on the glass as they watch us swimming around like brain-dead guppies in our grief.

Liz Winters showed up as if she has anything to offer other than blabbing about how we all used to be on the ski team together. And how one time you shared a room during a meet. She seems to have forgotten she's the reason you and your dad barely talk. That you two hated each other.

Everyone's crying.

Teachers you didn't even HAVE are crying from the back pew, saying things like you were too young to go and how it's so tragic you never got a chance to shine.

You did shine though. You radiated shine.

And people you barely knew shed tears. Like Spencer Jordon, a guy in my AP Chem class. Like he's jumping on some bandwagon of grief.

There are lilies covering your casket. Lilies. They're white.

I can't stop thinking about the time you said neutral colors made you sad because white isn't even a color but a shade and that any color is better than a shade.

Your aunt sang "If I Die Young" twice, because once wasn't enough sobbing for the entire crowd of people lining the walls of Saint Christopher's.

The photo of us your mom took right before school started is blown up next to your casket. Only I'm cropped out. And no one knows that smile on your face is forced because we were eating popcorn and watching Booksmart for the ten thousandth time talking about how we *were* them when your mom came in and made us smile for a picture. And we made her take it three times so we could get our angles right.

And Cade. He's here with his dad, and he keeps looking over at me with the saddest expression. I-broke-up-with-you pity doesn't hold a candle to your-best-friend-died pity.

I hate this.

I miss you, you asshole.

WHAT I DON'T SAY

There is no sun today.

But there is this beautiful stained-glass window behind Vanessa's coffin that would be even more stunning if rays of sunshine were cast through it. However, it's winter and the sky is more fog than anything, and it feels like it's because she's gone. How can there be light in my world when the brightest human in it is gone?

I stand for ten minutes at the entrance to the church, trying to figure out where I should be sitting—with my moms in the back by the door, or up close next to Mr. and Mrs. Carson and Mason. Luckily someone ushers me right up front between Mason and the Carsons.

Her mom looks smaller than she did last week. Her hair isn't straightened or gloriously long with a bright silver streak. It's packed into a lazy bun at the nape of her neck, like showering was the last thing on her mind this morning. Her eyelids are red and paper thin, and she's so broken and brittle people hug her like she's made of glass.

The way her father is silent as stone, I wonder if he feels bad that everything was always a fight. That he was the reason she escaped into books and quit the ski team, and hated being at home. He doesn't sob the way her mom does, but he also doesn't look up when the priest gives the eulogy. No one does.

The mascara hasn't even dried on her cheeks when Mrs. Carson begins sobbing in a noiseless, aching way that makes my soul turn inside out. She looks as if she got the chance to stop breathing, she'd take it.

And Mason, *Vanessa's* Mason, who buries his face into my shoulder so hard I think I'll feel the stain of his tears forever. My stomach clenches every time I feel his body shudder into me because I know that he's hurting just as much as I am.

Kat-Mom says that grief comes in waves, because if you had to feel it all at once, it would be too much. And today it is Mason's turn.

I know I should cry. I know I'm supposed to cry. But here with all the people who don't even know about Vanessa's real laugh—the one that made her snort like a Boston terrier. A genuine belly laugh, not at all the giggle she released in a video about her Book Boyfriend of the Week. Characters she dreamed about, that felt so real to her I sometimes forgot she was talking about people who lived only in pages.

There's a hole as quiet as death in my heart—it's been hollowed out by the explosion of Vanessa's car. The empty cavern is now just a graveyard for the shrapnel in my bones.

She can't be gone.

A week ago she was alive.

A week ago she was a book girl who was writing the novel of her life.

She wasn't done.

We weren't done.

RECEPTION

Mr. and Mrs. Carson chose to have "If I Die Young" played for a third time as we're all ushered out. Vanessa's been sent away with the words of a love song—only there's no bed of roses. Her casket was closed, but I know she's lying on emerald-green satin.

The reception area boasts a spread of bland catered food and funeral programs filled with poems and scriptures she likely never connected with. There are so many people here, they run out of the pamphlets by the time I get out. Luckily, I find one abandoned near the deviled eggs Mrs. Carson spent a nauseating amount of time picking out with the caterer.

My moms insist I make a plate, but I don't feel like eating.

Instead, I stand silently with Mason near the back door, watching people in line tell Mr. and Mrs. Carson things like "I'm so sorry for your loss" and "Let us know if you need anything." As if there is anything they could do or say to take away the fact that their only child is dead.

When Cade steps into line with his dad to pay his respects, my heart feels like it's going to swell out of my chest. Seeing him here shouldn't feel awkward. A few months ago we were all inseparable, a team, the four of us. And now we're in ruins.

"This is so screwed up," Mason whispers next to me. I turn, and he's staring down at his paint-splotch-covered shoes. Chin trembling as a sound comes out of his mouth that reminds of me of a video I watched once in biology of a rabbit screaming. It's strangled and all wrong, and I wish I could forget it.

I start to say something, but Mason's lips are tight, and he's shaking his head like he's willing me to stop speaking altogether. I know better than anyone how he feels—congruent lines with the same intersection of grief. Vanessa.

"Bailey, it's all—" And I know in my heart what he's going to say next. It's all his fault. It's all our fault. I know because it's the same thing that pops into my mind if I leave myself with my thoughts for too long.

"Don't finish that sentence," I say, eyes darting to his, begging him to stop. He pauses, hesitating before he resolves with a nod, disappearing from my side and darting across the room before Liz stops him.

She looks fresh off the trails, with a slight pink hue to her cheeks. With the Ski Squad behind her, Liz almost looks nice. Her friends, the ones who used to be our friends. The way Liz's hand moves to his back, rubbing it while the other sits on her heart. Seeing her comfort Mason is almost enough to make me forget how awful she was to us.

When I turn back to the line, Cade joins me, clearing his throat twice before saying my name. He says it with the same apology-stained voice he used the last time we *really* spoke—in his car during lunch

72

just days after he ended it out of nowhere. Those same impossibly blue eyes are swollen with red rims; his face is splotched bright red.

I know this face too.

"Thanks for coming," I say.

"Bailey." He swallows my name this time, like it's sharp in his throat.

"I know," I say. Because after a year together, I know what comes next is an "I'm sorry," and if he says it out loud, I won't be able to hold it together. I reach down between us and grab his hand so he stops talking. It's sweaty and hot, but after a beat he slides his fingers in with mine.

When he turns into me, pulling me to the spot under his arm that used to feel as warm as a blanket straight out of the dryer, I break. My chin falls, tucking into the corner of his neck, where I feel him whisper, "I'm so, so sorry."

And Cade holds me for a long time, and we watch as Mr. and Mrs. Carson console others less deserving of their grief. Vanessa would have laughed, that sad sardonic laugh, seeing them side by side. A united front, when behind closed doors, their home was never a happy one.

DEATH OF A QUIET BOOK GIRL

This wasn't the first time Vanessa died.

See, Vanessa used to be a quiet book girl. Even after she caught her dad cheating—and told her mom, and her parents almost divorced twice—she was content to live out her rage within the pages of her books and fan fiction.

Everyone in town knows Mr. Carson, and what kind of man he is. A two-time gold medalist in cross-country skiing. Just ask him, he'll tell you. He's the first on the trails in the morning, and the last off them. A renowned ski coach as long as I can remember, and before I met Vanessa, I met Mr. C when my parents dropped me off for my very first lesson.

I used to tell Vanessa how I liked the way cross-country skiing made me feel like I was flying, even if Mr. Carson used to call us "ski participants"—the people who lingered in the back—not like "real" skiers. Like Liz, the new girl from Kenai, and her Ski Squad posse. Until that year, Vanessa didn't mind because she didn't care about the sport as much as she cared about books.

Every year since we were little, the Carsons threw a huge Christmas party. A small band, a giant Martha Stewart–inspired tree, the works. And the year we started high school was no different. Same party, same music, but a brand-new fireplace and flooring as a result of the very first "I'm sorry" remodel. And the first year Liz's family attended.

There was a lot to celebrate, I guess. Mr. Carson had followed us up to the high school team. He was really jazzed about it, and why wouldn't he be? Liz was killing every meet, coming in first in nearly every event.

So Mr. Carson drank until he slurred, tipping his glass of whisky to the sky during his annual toast. He boasted, talking about how this year was going to be incredible, in no small part because Liz was part of his team now. He even joked that she was the daughter he never had. Going on to elaborate "because the girl can ski," and it was the kind of talent he'd been waiting his whole career to coach.

It was one of those moments where you can imagine a record scratch. A halt to all the fun and games as Mr. Carson realized what he'd said, and Mrs. Carson stared on in disbelief. Even Liz turned her eyes to the ground, afraid to look at anyone.

But Vanessa didn't look away. No, she stared right into her father's eyes. And even as the music started up and Mr. Carson excused himself for a moment, she never lost the impish smile on her face.

Because that was the day the quiet book girl died. If it were written between pages, it would have been her origin story—the beginning of her transformation from quiet book girl in the back of class who never spoke out of turn, to wild book girl. Vibrant book girl. Never-took-no-for-an-answer girl.

At first Vanessa wasn't even mad. She was the quiet book girl then, remember. That was her cue to push herself, and push herself she did. She skipped yearbook and creative writing club to hit a second practice every day—even on weekends.

Weekends.

Because if there was one thing Vanessa wanted, it was to prove to her father that he was wrong about her, just as much as he wanted to prove to her that she was wrong about him.

The day of the big meet, Vanessa had fire in her feet. She pushed herself harder than I'd ever seen her push before. She was behind Liz, just by a few feet—skis swooshing against the grain of the snow, arms outstretched. Vanessa was flying, free forward, her cheeks puffing in and out.

When she attempted to pass Liz, something happened. Her footing missed, and Vanessa was skis-up in the air, legs twisted the entire wrong way, and the whole crowd gasped as she tried to get up.

Liz didn't even stop.

At the hospital I held her hand when the doctor showed her family the X-ray. Vanessa's leg was broken in two separate spots and Mr. Carson didn't miss a beat before asking how long it would be before she could ski again.

"I hate you," Vanessa said, and the doctor and nurse and everyone else in the room stopped to look at her. She was so mad her fingers went white as she gripped the sheets of that ER gurney–turned-bed. She cut into him, right there in front of everyone. "If you can't love me off skis then you don't love me at all."

After that we didn't ski anymore.

And we didn't talk to Liz anymore either.

Because that's the kind of friends we were. We always, always had each other's backs.

It was three weeks later when Mr. Carson brought in Tundra Cove's finest, Jordon Contracting, for Vanessa's very own "I'm sorry" remodel—the floor-to-ceiling bookcases, designer bed frame, and reclaimed wood desk. Proof he could love her even if she didn't ski.

Bailey: Okay. Finally home.

Let's get this started.

V: get what started?

long day?

Bailey: Okay, okay. Lowercase.

Seems like this is working.

V: earth to bailey.

what the hell are you talking about?

Bailey: Sorry.

Like I was saying. It's been a long day, but it's better now.

I've got you back.

V: damn right.

so what happened?

Bailey: Doesn't matter.

V: ok weirdo.

Bailey: The night of the party you said you were going to meet Mason.

V: i was at your house, ya silly!

remember?

pop rocks.

booksmart?

i skipped a whole thing!

78

Bailey: Oh I remember.

But then you said you had to go.

That you were going to get Mason.

Somehow you ended up on the pass.

V: i . . .

i don't remember.

who takes the pass?

there's nothing up there.

Bailey: There's nothing up there.

Wait, no, there is.

We've taken the pass before.

I know I've seen houses.

V: well yeah.

houses.

but no one we know.

what's the deal, bailey?

GOOGLE MAPS

There are five homes that come up in my search.

One belongs to an Ash and Travis Mitchell. They're in their thirties and live off the grid. Their blog about living sustainably through winter has like a million followers and apparently he's a wizard with sourdough.

A bank-owned foreclosure available for purchase. Based on the pictures online, it's unlivable.

Another vacant home, but this one was purchased earlier in the year. I can't figure out who owns it; property details are vague. Based on photos it looks huge—apparently some old billionaire built it in the seventies. There's a hot tub in the middle of one of the three (yes, three) living rooms and whoever bought it has their work cut out for them.

A bed-and-breakfast with gorgeous pictures. They even have a wedding venue barn attached, and the couple that lives there seems awesome. Her name is Claudia Bishop and she does all the wedding planning stuff while her husband, Alex, is one of Alaska's top-rated photographers.

Lastly, one with a huge family. After looking up the owners in the property records, and stalking them on Facebook, I found out that they're super religious and homeschool all seven (yes, seven) of their children. They have one teen close to our age. Edward Miller. He's cute. According to my research, he does community theater here in Tundra Cove and has quite the singing voice, but after scouring his social media I don't see any connection whatsoever with Vanessa.

Bailey: Okay new question.

V: here for it.

Bailey: Do you know Edward Miller?

V: nope.

never heard of him.

Bailey: Claudia Bishop?

Alex Bishop?

V: no and no.

Bailey: Ash or Travis Mitchell?

And your pin.

V: pin?

Bailey: The one from Forget Me Always.

Where is it?

V: you're being weird again.

Bailey: Wait.

Of course you don't know who these people are.

If we haven't talked about them, you wouldn't know them.

V: yes, exactly. told you i tell you everything.

Bailey: Hey Cade

Thank you for coming today. It meant a lot to me.

DO NOT ANSWER: I wouldn't have missed it

Bailey: It was good to see you too.

DO NOT ANSWER: It was good to see u too.

Are u going to school 2morrow?

I can give u a ride

Bailey: I don't think.

I'm not ready.

Mason: You awake?

Bailey: Yes.

Mason: Can't sleep.

Today was a lot.

Sorry if I was acting weird.

Bailey: Don't worry about it.

I don't think there's any normal way to act at a funeral.

They suck.

Mason: That was hard.

No good music.

No excerpts from her favorite books.

Everyone wearing black.

Bailey: She hated shades—colors only.

Mason: Exactly.

It didn't feel like it was for her.

Bailey: Yeah.

Mason: I keep wondering how this could happen.

This can't be real.

Bailey: I've been texting her. That's helped.

Mason: I called her voicemail like three times this morning
to hear her voice before I could get out of bed.

I'd give anything to talk to her one more time.

Bailey: Me too.

You have no idea.

WEEK THREE

A NEW DAY

"You heal when you sleep."

It's something Kat-Mom always says but hasn't felt true until I woke up this morning.

Today I actually feel rested.

Like maybe I can go to school because the longer I wait, the harder it'll be. The longer I wait, the weirder people will treat me. The longer I wait, the harder it'll be without Vanessa there.

I throw on some clothes, but I'm still half-awake when I hear my moms' voices downstairs, the whir of the coffee machine grinding beans, and the fridge door opening and closing. I wash my face and even moisturize with some hippie lotion Kat-Mom swears by that smells like sage and rosemary and lemon all at once. By the time I run a brush through the matted hair at the nape of my neck, I'm ready to crawl back in bed, but I keep moving.

Keep going.

And when I get downstairs, I don't wait for them to look at me before I say, "I've got school today."

Kat-Mom's mouth parts, like she's trying to find words. Jacky-Mom closes her laptop and takes off her glasses, and I pretend I don't notice the way they're trying to have one of those telepathic momversations right there in front of me.

"You don't have to," Kat-Mom says. "You can take as much time as you want."

"I know." I flash a smile entirely for show. "I want to go back. I imagine I'm pretty far behind. Plus, I've got to keep my grades up. I can't very well expect a college to take my transcripts seriously if I drop the ball at this point."

I sit down just like I would have before the accident. I grab a muffin, and Kat-Mom hands me a cup of coffee, while Jacky-Mom asks if I want the peppermint-flavored creamer she usually hoards.

They pretend it's normal, and so it is. At least for this one small part of the day, it's okay.

Bailey: I guess it's time for me to get a driver's license.

V: what? and ruin your misguided belief that you don't actually need to drive in high school?

Bailey: Hey. That system has been fairly effective thus far.

V: yeah.

because you mooch rides off me and cade.

Bailey: Mooched*

V: fine. mooched.

so why are you in sudden need of a driver's license?

Bailey: It's kind of funny.

Today I got ready to go to school, went downstairs, and had breakfast with moms.

And it was fine, they were fine, but I kept waiting for you to walk through the door and steal the last bagel and go on about the book you read last night.

V: that does sound like me.

Bailey: And then Jacky-Mom kept looking at the clock in the kitchen. Kat-Mom was downing her cup of coffee and reaching for her keys yelling about how they were going to be late when they both stopped and looked at me.

V: classic pierce-anderson household antics.

Bailey: Then it hit them all at once that I would need a ride.

V: i can come get you!

Bailey: No. It's fine.

V: absolutely not.

give me ten minutes.

Bailey: I'd like that.

I'd like that a whole lot.

IN A PERFECT WORLD

There's another timeline somewhere.

Vanessa didn't die. And she picked me up for school today the same way she did every day before that. We got coffee on the way— my Americano and her "whatever the special is"—and I paid because she drives me everywhere. She turned on a playlist she'd curated for winter and we hummed along with the songs until pulling into the school parking lot.

In that timeline I don't have to pull out all the winter gear I kept from when we were still on the ski team—my thick white beanie with the fur pom, my old gloves with the Tundra Cove High School husky on the cuff, and the fleece-lined Sorel boots I only use every few months now because I almost never venture out into winter anymore.

My lungs don't fill up with cold, and I don't think for a moment that I kind of miss wearing a mask everywhere I go because at least it kept my face warm. The crunch of snow against the studs in my

93

boots doesn't remind me of the way our skis used to click against the ice, and I don't smile because I sort of missed that sound.

The biggest difference in these timelines is that I don't walk all the way to school, past whitened tree limbs and frost-covered homes. And my tears never freeze on my lashes before they can meet my cheeks.

HERE AND NOW

My whole face is numb by the time I get to school. I breeze through the arctic entry, a warm fan blasting down over my body as I kick my boots against the metal grate underfoot. Ahead, in the school, it's quiet. I'm late, so everyone's in their classrooms when the bell rings, living their lives like nothing ever happened.

Like she never happened.

Then Tundra Cove High comes to life in front of me. Crowds form in the hallways, people gathered around lockers and sharing inside jokes and laughing about things that really aren't important. Not in the long run. The front office is bustling with admin assistants and office aides talking, chattering about this or that.

There's a moment amid the chaos when it feels like any other school day. That's the kind of chaos I live for. The fluorescent overhead lights lead the way down the hall to my locker, a beacon promising that once I get there, the weight of the last few weeks might disappear.

I'm almost to my locker when I see a group of girls lean into one another and whisper. It's Liz and the rest of the Ski Squad, probably talking about whatever stupid party they hit up once everyone left the funeral. They move out of my way like crabs on the beach, scuttling aside.

Liz's eyes gloss over me as they pass, and I swear she's about to say something, but her lips tighten at the last second like she's thought better of it. I stop in my tracks when I see Vanessa's locker right next to mine, letting my backpack drop off my shoulder onto the floor with a thud that reverberates through the hall.

But what's in front of me doesn't even *look* like her locker.

MESSAGES WRITTEN ON HER LOCKER

"I'll keep your memory alive" —Teddy Stenson

Who is this?

"RIP VERONICA"

Seriously? Veronica?

They couldn't even get her name right.

"you were the best friend." —Brianne Bridges

Best. Friend. Funny—such good friends and we only ever hung out with her at the occasional dance and parties.

"I can't believe you won't be here anymore. We love you, Vanessa. Gone too soon."

Bandwagon grief at its finest.

Sure, there are some beautiful messages. Like one that says "I'll miss you forever" from her favorite teacher, Mrs. Hendricks, or the one my AP Chem partner, Esther, wrote about how she'll always remember her kindness.

But the rest of them, with the flowers and pictures printed off from Vanessa's social media accounts, make my heart feel ten times heavier.

Like they were the ones who grew up whispering in each other's ears and had years' worth of data from texts saved on their phones. Notes that chronicle every time they fought and had to type it all out, save it, and read it before they actually hit "send."

The story of our friendship is recorded in person, in photograph, online.

Their friendship is temporary. Promised only on butcher paper, meant for cheerleaders and the pep squad to put up in hallways before hockey games and spirit week—now taped to her locker. As fleeting as every copy of the school newsletter that ends up in the bottom of every wastebasket.

A lie to attach themselves to grief that belongs to me and like three other people.

THE ABOMINATION

Even after everyone disappears to their classes, I'm still here.

Like in movies where a character is stuck in time while everyone runs around them in super-speed. I'm standing there, motionless while the entire world keeps going on.

"Crazy, right?" I turn to see Mason gesturing to the locker shrine. He pulls a hood from his head, fingernails stained black and green from paint. For a second we stand there, just a couple of people with a lot of feelings, and no one saying any of them.

"Yeah." I shake my head, taking off my hat and unwrapping the scarf from around my neck. I step forward, kneeling down to really look at the whole thing. Shaking my head, I twist my scarf in my hands. Unease sweeps over me and I look back to him. "Crazy."

I'm numb again, coming to a stand. A hundred different things to say pop into my head, but I can't force anything off my tongue. Instead, I stare into his big brown eyes, which are so intently focused on the locker. He looks like a little boy almost, just as lost in the messages as I was a moment ago.

His thick brows lower and his breath hitches before his gaze turns to me, picking up where we left off at the funeral, and I can feel it.

"Mason, do you know where—"

"—stop." Every hair on my arms stands on end as he cuts me off. A wave of unease swells through my stomach, and I wish I were the type of person who could barrel over him and finish that sentence. I want to know if he's seen her pin, because maybe wherever it is will be a clue to where she was going that night.

He swallows his words, blinking back what I can only guess are tears.

"Bailey, we can both do the what-if game forever. What if I didn't ask her to meet me at her house? What if you weren't tex—" Mason's face twists up like he's trying to unspeak the words he just said. "I'm sorry—I meant . . ."

"I know what you meant." I force my gaze on him.

"We can't live like this forever. We'll probably never know what happened that night, so dwelling on it doesn't do anyone any good."

And in my heart, I know he's right, but it doesn't stop me from wanting to know where she was going that night. From wanting to know how her favorite pin went missing from her favorite jacket. From needing to know more than I need to breathe. What took her up that hill, and was it worth dying for?

PARADISE LOST

I used to love everything about AP Chem.

I love the periodic table of elements on the back wall and the beakers lined up in the glass cabinet doors. I even love how it smells like equal parts cleaning solution and rubber, which most people probably hate about this class but I enjoy.

How when we were together, Cade and I always walked in holding hands. And during class, we'd link our pinkies under the table while he'd write cute messages in the margins of my notes. For the first semester, Esther (who wasn't my partner then) would only call him "Bailey's boyfriend" and he never corrected her.

Mrs. Kamaka doesn't comment that I walked in five minutes late, and I keep my head down because I'm afraid if I don't, she'll give me pity eyes. The last thing I want are pity eyes.

She extends her tattooed arm across the length of the board while I walk to my seat, and she keeps going on with her lesson. I lift my gaze to the table where I used to sit with Cade, but since the breakup I sit with Esther.

I pass Cade and *his* new partner—Spencer Jordon—aka the guy Cade rolled his eyes at every time Spencer's hand went up so he could "just circle back around" to something that Mrs. K said. Back when we were together, Cade would complain that he couldn't understand how Spencer even got into AP Chem because he was so stupid.

I used to tell Cade I didn't think he was all that bad, but after seeing Spencer lead the bandwagon of grief at Vanessa's funeral, I'm reserving my right to also dislike him.

My eyes lock with Cade, my chest tightening as his expression shifts into a weak smile.

Esther smiles in that warm way she always does, scooting in as I usher myself next to her. She shrugs, tucking into the fur-lined coat she's wearing, beaded earrings dangling from her ears. "Welcome back."

"Thanks," I whisper, setting my book on the table and opening it to the page listed on the whiteboard and wondering what would happen if I got up right now and walked out of class and all the way home to my computer so I could grill V about where she was going that night.

"I took notes while you were gone," she whispers back, sliding a few pages to me filled with perfectly scrawled handwriting. I nod, forcing a grin as if it doesn't feel like my face is burning red.

I'm there in class. I'm doing the assignment, jumping right into the lesson plan like I should, but my mind is stuck back on that night, wondering which pieces I missed, what part I must have misremembered.

DO NOT ANSWER: Hey.

Bailey: Hey.

DO NOT ANSWER: I didn't think u were coming today.

Bailey: Me either.

I have regrets.

Starting with the walk here.

DO NOT ANSWER: Too soon?

Bailey: That's an understatement.

The locker shrine was a lot.

And I'm stuck.

DO NOT ANSWER: ya.

I get it.

Bailey: Sorry I'm a mess.

I thought I could do this, but I can't.

I need to go home.

DO NOT ANSWER: u need a ride?

Bailey: I'm okay.

DO NOT ANSWER: let me drive u.

It's cold.

Bailey: But school.

DO NOT ANSWER: My dad won't care.

Bailey: okay.

Bailey: Can you call the office and excuse me for the rest of the day?

Jacky-Mom: Are you okay?

Kat-Mom: yes of course.

Bailey: Yeah.

I just didn't realize how hard it was going to be.

I'll email all my teachers and get my assignments.

Kat-Mom: We aren't worried about you getting behind, honey.

Take the time you need.

We love you.

Jacky-Mom: I'm emailing the admin now.

Kat-Mom: I'll come home as soon as I'm done with my last client.

Bailey: Thanks moms.

Love you.

Kat-Mom: Love you too.

Jacky-Mom: ♥

FAMILIAR

When we broke up, I took every memory of Cade out of my room.

I started by replacing my sheets. They were blue, like his eyes, and every time I saw them I thought about all the times we took advantage of my parents being out of the house and wrapped ourselves in them. Then it was the bouquet of dried flowers hanging in the corner of my room—he got them for me "just because" last year and Vanessa told me I had to dry them and keep them forever. Then, when those were gone, I went for the weird wax mold of us holding hands that we made at the fair.

After my room was Cade-free, Kat-Mom saged the shit out of it.

It's muscle memory to turn to him as he pulls into the driveway—after a whole car ride of small talk about how his dad is doing and if he's going to get a job next summer before college—and ask if he wants to come in. Cade hesitates at first, because of course he does.

This is weird.

And we walk into the house, slipping our shoes off, and standing nervously like we weren't friends for years before we knew what each other's tongues tasted like. Having him back here feels like reinstalling a virus after it's completely depleted your hard drive. And the way he walks into my room, looking around like he's searching for part of himself, makes me feel strangely self-conscious.

"You got a new computer?" he asks.

"For my birthday." I cringe. My desk is littered with chaos. A half-empty bag of popcorn from last night and three empty water bottles stacked up next to my laptop. Vanessa's jacket is still where she left it, draped over the back of my ergonomically designed computer chair, like she's going to pop in to pick it up any minute now.

"Right." His eyes move over to my bed and back to me.

My shoulders rise and fall with a breath and I don't even bother finishing the sentence. Clearly holding his hand at the funeral wasn't a problem, and talking to him through a screen is fine, but in person is like I'm trying to edit a warped file with all the wrong software.

"I wanted to talk to you after," he blurts out, and he's standing awkwardly at the edge of my room. "But I don't know how you're feeling about everything and if it would be . . ."

"Messed up?" I finish the sentence for him, cringing. Two words that seem to sum up my existence these last few weeks, and when I say them out loud, my insides feel like my brain's under a microscope and he can see my every thought.

"I was going to say weird." His lips part in a thin smile. "You said you were stuck?"

"Yeah." I stare over at the computer on my desk, where V is just sitting, waiting for me to message her. He grabs my hand, rubbing his thumb against my palm the way he used to whenever he was trying to show me he was listening.

"She left here that night, and said she was going home. Mason was leaving that Zoe's party to meet her there. And somehow, Vanessa ended up on the pass." I sort of laugh the last word, but in one of those hysterical ways like it's about to turn into a sob. "I just don't get it. And Mason—"

Cade's head tilts, listening intently, as I go on.

"He doesn't want to dwell on it. He doesn't think we'll ever really know how she ended up there." I shrug, thinking back to the picture Liz posted of herself. Her face, Mason's behind it, Cade looking off camera like he was in the middle of a conversation. "You saw Mason that night. Did he seem okay?"

Cade's shrugs, his hand slipping away from my mine to run through his hair. "I don't know, Bailey. I'll be honest. I don't remember much." It's not until his eyes move away from mine that I realize how crazy-ex-girlfriend I sound right now. Like I was intentionally keeping tabs on him.

I release a heavy sigh, folding my arms over my chest. Cade's expression changes, and he reaches for my hand again, and this time pulls me toward him.

"Hey. Bailey, c'mon. It's Mason." He wraps both arms around my shoulders and rests his chin on my head. His lungs make a swooshing sound as they fill with air, and I let myself melt into him, this familiar feeling, like we've rewound time and we're three months back, before the breakup, the accident, and everything was so backward I couldn't make sense of forward. "He's upset. Maybe he's feeling guilty because she was going to see him or something."

Maybe he's right.

Maybe Mason's in denial.

Maybe that's why he's not ready for answers yet.

I pull back, watching Cade's jaw soften and knowing what comes next and doing absolutely nothing to stop it because I want to remain rewound. My feet arch on tiptoes, and he bends down enough that our lips brush against each other in a tentative kiss.

Because everything is so messed up already, why not let it get a little messier?

Esther: I tried to find you after school but you were already gone.

I've got those notes if you want them.

Bailey: That would be awesome!

Esther: I can bring them over now. I have my mom's car today.

Bailey: Oh cool. I'll share my location.

Esther: See you soon!

Mason: Do you need a ride?

You still here?

Bailey: Sorry.

I went home early today.

Cade drove me.

Mason: Oh.

Cool.

no worries.

Bailey: thanks though.

Bailey: I can't talk long because Esther is bringing me homework BUT today has been WEIRD.

V: tell me about it.

i think i'm going to get bangs.

thoughts?

Bailey: See: the 9th grade bangs fiasco.

I think I have it in writing somewhere that I'm supposed to tell you that you're never supposed to entertain the idea of fringe again.

V: this is why we pay you the big bucks.

Bailey: And by big bucks you mean nothing.

V: exactly.

okay so what was weird?

Bailey: Well.

I'm glad you asked.

First things first.

I just got done making out with Cade.

V: oh shit.

Bailey: Turns out 3 months of being broken up is not enough time to make a random hookup not complicated.

V: was it hawt at least?

Bailey: NO.

I mean.

Yes. Very hawt.

Stupid hawt.

Also just stupid.

V: okay, yeah, you were right.

that does sound like a weird day.

Bailey: Then my moms came home and I think I got in trouble?

V: whoa!

why?

Bailey: Well I sort of told them I was feeling weird at school so they excused my absence, but then they saw me and Cade on the door camera when we walked up.

I kinda forgot we even had the stupid thing.

V: oooooh damn.

Bailey: So that was a nice awkward conversation with my mothers about how coming home from school is fine, but I can't share sick days in my room with my ex-boyfriend.

V: that does sound complicated.

but it was hawt?

stupid hawt?

Bailey: Yep.

And kinda sad?

V: good ole grief kissing.

are you getting back together?

Bailey: I don't know!

We made out.

Then he left.

V: did he text you after?

Bailey: Is he supposed to?

V: well usually there's some obligatory post-make-out flirtation that occurs after a random hookup.

ESTHER SMILES

Her dimpled grin is permanent.

And it makes my moms smile too when they show up and she's sitting at our dining room table. They pretend it's not weird I have someone here who I've never had over before. Not that they don't know Esther. Everyone in town knows the Greys; they're practically an institution in Tundra Cove, and her dad owns a diner down the hill boasting the best Tater Tots in Alaska.

Esther is quiet and shy, but when she does talk it's always to say something incredibly smart or kind. She's going to be the valedictorian, and everyone knows it—not because she brags, but because she's in every AP course, and even has a class that technically begins before school starts.

When my moms go into their room, she whispers, "I'm nervous," and when I ask why she says, "Your mom is so cool." I know she means Jacky-Mom, whose first baby was NewVision. Since then, she's been featured in countless tech magazines and publications. Last year she even did a TED Talk about machine-learning capabilities.

Still, I ask "Which one?" and we both laugh, my first genuine laugh since Vanessa died. It feels strange, strangled almost, and Esther must notice the way I hesitate after. Guilt. Like it shouldn't be so easy to laugh.

"Vanessa was really nice," she says. "I'm—I'm so sorry for your loss."

"Thanks," I manage, unsure what to even say in response. "I miss her so much."

"Last year my auntie died unexpectedly," Esther says, doodling a cross in her notebook. "The hardest part was not getting to say goodbye. No chance to ask her all the things I wish I could have asked when she was alive—like why she's so good at making earrings or how she makes her fry bread so tasty."

I slip away. I'm stuck again. "Did she have secrets too?"

"Oh, that doesn't matter." Esther has a sparkle in her dark brown eyes, and an impish shrug, as she says, "It's not the secrets that matter when people we love die, but the memories we keep in our hearts."

See? When Esther speaks, it's to say something incredibly smart, and incredibly kind.

GOOGLE SEARCH HISTORY

Do traumatic events effect memory?

What's the difference between effect and affect?

"Vanessa Carson Obituary"

"Vanessa Carson" Alaska

"Vanessa Carson" social media

What does it mean when you kiss your ex?

Mason: You up?

Bailey: Yeah.

Mason: I can't sleep.

Bailey: Me either.

Esther came over today and she was here late helping me with homework.

Mason: Hook up with the brainiac. Smart.

Bailey: One might argue that I am also a brainiac.

Mason: I meant she was smart for pairing up with you. ;)

Bailey: Oh.

Then thanks.

Anyway.

It was weird.

Hanging out with someone who isn't Vanessa.

Mason: I bet.

You were tight.

I have a lot of friends.

But I've never had a best friend like that.

I mean one that wasn't also my girlfriend.

Bailey: I know you get it.

Mason: You know what helps?

Bailey: A lobotomy?

Mason: That was dark.

I was going to say watch some Bob Ross.

So relaxing.

Bailey: Are you serious right now?

Mason: Yeah.

You have Netflix right?

Bailey: Yes. I'm not a grandma.

Mason: Turn it on. Right now. I'll start over.

Bailey: Bob Ross.

Mason: Bob Ross.

Bailey: Like, we're literally going to watch paint dry.

Mason: Trust me. It's relaxing as hell.

Bailey: FINE.

Only because I have nothing better to do.

THE REAL MASON

By the time I get Netflix pulled up on my laptop, find Bob Ross, and scroll down to the first episode, my phone is buzzing. I look down to see Mason's name flashing across the screen.

The last time he called me was the second time he'd ever called me—the night she died. Not that there was ever a reason to while Vanessa was alive. It feels all wrong as I swipe right, answering, and pull the phone to my ear.

"Is it common practice to call people in the middle of the night?" I half whisper.

"When you're both up and watching Bob Ross, it absolutely is." I can hear a smile in his voice as I settle beneath my weighted blanket. It all feels so strangely taboo, talking to my best friend's boyfriend in a hushed whisper after midnight, but the feeling quickly disappears when I imagine Mason on the other end of the phone.

He sounds so lonely, and I know—like I know way too many other things about Mason—that being lonely is the worst thing he can feel.

"Can you talk?"

"Yeah, press play now." I ditch the whisper. There's no way my moms can hear from the basement floor, and even if they could, they wouldn't likely care. Vanessa and I used to stay up all the time talking on the phone, talking in person, having late-night movie marathons with the TV blaring.

Bob Ross isn't about to wake anyone up.

The episode starts, funky eighties music at the beginning and vibrant lettering that shifts as Bob appears with his signature poof of hair and a palette in his hands. He starts off with the colors he'll be using—there are only four, but Bob doesn't care—and he's all cool and breezy, dipping the first brush in and scattering paint across the page.

"Wait, so he's going to do this whole thing with four colors?" It's too awkward to sit on the phone in silence.

"He only needs four colors," Mason says. "Did you know Bob Ross was stationed up here too? He was a drill sergeant at Fort Eielson."

"That can't be right." I try to imagine his voice as anything but smooth like honey.

We continue watching. Bob has put on the base, moving to mountains and filling in texture where needed. He's so eerily calm about everything as he encourages viewers not to worry about how much paint to use. He's dipping his brush in the green, mixing in just a dab of blue, when Mason says, "Oh look, a happy little tree."

The word *happy* buries the conversation. Like we can both feel the weight of the word, the juxtaposition, the reason why we are even talking on the phone. Why we're watching some show about painting to forget why we're both up this late, and alone, to begin with.

"How are you?" Mason asks. His voice seems raspier at night.

"I miss her."

"Me too," he says. And I'm so grateful when I hear him jumping into the episode again. "Oh! Oh, do you see that? More happy trees! I bet anything there's a—" Bob Ross is already finishing the sentence via the delay. "A happy little squirrel in that tree!"

"You're ridiculous," I say, smiling at the sound of Mason chuckling at his own joke on the other end of the phone—and it sounds a little like bees buzzing. And he's right, it does take my mind off of everything for a little.

Just a little.

WEEK FOUR

THE THINGS WE REMEMBER

I stay home another three days. Jacky-Mom stays home with me, working from her office while I "do homework" and play with the app. The reality is, I'm blasting through the assignments with almost no effort, getting marginal scores because I'm too busy working on the app.

Going through every social media post Vanessa ever made, every private message we shared, and transferring them to V. Tweaking the code, updating my own knowledge by scanning resources online instead of putting my efforts into killing this semester. My last semester.

I feel bad for lying to them, but I can't get the images of Jacky-Mom's thin-lipped annoyed face and Kat-Mom's "I wish you'd have come to me" frown out of my head.

After dinner one night, they share a glance as Jacky-Mom asks me to stay before I can disappear to my room the way I've been doing every night this week.

"We wanted to check in and see how you're feeling about every-thing," Kat-Mom says, and I know that therapizing tone better than anyone.

These are the times I really wish I weren't an only child. It'd be pretty stellar if there was literally any other person to take up their time or energy. It was one of the things Vanessa and I always bonded over. The pain of being an only child and having all our parents focused on one kid.

"I'm okay," I say. "Sad."

Jacky-Mom nods, hesitant before asking, "When do you think you'll go back to school?"

And there's a lot we say after. How I promise I'll go back on Monday, and they think that's a good amount of time. Kat-Mom tells me it's hard to lose friends at any age, but when you're a teen and it's your best friend therapy therapy therapy words. I know what she's saying probably makes a lot of sense, but I don't want to hear it.

It's when Jacky-Mom pops in with "You have other friends too" and "What about Esther" and "You can't shut yourself off from your responsibilities" that I feel the bristly anger bubbling up in my stomach—angry bile at the back of my throat I have to push down before responding.

"It was different with her. She was my *best* friend." Vanessa was the only person in my whole life I'd ever called that, and I can't imagine using that term for anyone else. "Sorry if I'm not ready to move on from a perfect friendship."

And Kat-Mom smiles, threading a finger through the ends of my hair. "Oh, Bailey, it's so easy to only remember the good when people go. That's important. But you can't forget that she was human. You have to remember that nothing and no one is perfect."

Bailey: What would you say was our biggest fight ever?

V: the electives debate of 10th grade.

hands down.

Bailey: Forgive me for wanting a single class with my BEST FRIEND.

V: oh wait.

no.

masongate.

Bailey: What?

V: for sure.

it was the night mason showed up at my window while we were having a sleepover.

Bailey: TO BE FAIR

It was supposed to be a girls' night.

Implication being that there was no boy there.

Then all of a sudden he shows up and taps on your window and you were all oooooo it's Mason.

V: you could have stayed.

Bailey: Ew.

V: what?

Bailey: IT'S NOT LIKE HE WAS THERE TO HANG OUT AND WATCH A MOVIE.

V: oh no.

don't start.

yes he was.

Bailey: Doubt it.

And it wasn't that I was mad he was there.

I was just sad.

V: what?

why?

Bailey: I don't know.

It was the first time I felt like he might be more important to you than me.

V: nah.

boys come and go. you're my forever.

I REMEMBER

I'd been trying to hang out for a while.

Vanessa was busy, though, and something with her parents always came up last minute, or she had a project due for some class, and way too many times it was because she had some volunteer something or other she had to attend. It wasn't all her either. It was our sophomore year. My first in debate, and the STEM Club I'd started the year before took up a lot of time.

Still, it wasn't like I couldn't *find* time for her.

And when Mason showed up out of nowhere it felt like a kick to the stomach.

He smelled stale that night, like every party I'd ever been to where rancid beer mixed with sweat, smelling like the worst combination of hockey gear and trash can. He did a little tumble off the bed from the window and she crawled closer to the edge to kiss him. It wasn't even one of those long passionate kisses—they weren't making out or anything—but it sucked the life out of me to see her drop me for him so quick.

Then he reached under her bed and pulled out a green duffel bag—my heart sank as she reminded him to be quiet while he threw the bag over his shoulder and disappeared into the bathroom with an "I know, I know" like this is something they did all the time.

He was comfortable in her room.

"What the hell?" I whispered, grabbing my backpack and stuffing my pillow in. "If your parents knew he was here you'd be dead!" I added as soon as I heard the bathroom fan turn on.

"Bailey, wait—no, you should stay."

"No. I'm not going to sit here and hang out while you and Mason—" I stopped, letting my mind go to literally the only reason Mason would be stumbling, drunk, into her room at midnight. It was a booty call.

"Did you have sex?" I asked, without even thinking about the way it sounded.

"Bailey, that's not why he's here." Her pencil-perfect eyebrows lifted when she was upset, forming a straight line across her forehead.

"You had sex?" I couldn't help the hurt in my voice. The twinge of sadness. I waited for her to argue, but when she didn't, I softened. My best friend, my person, didn't think she could tell me. "Why didn't you say anything?"

I couldn't stop thinking about all the firsts between us. The first time she kissed whatshisface in ninth grade just a few weeks before she and Mason started dating. Or when Cade asked me if he could kiss me while studying like a week into school. How both times we texted immediately. How every single first before this was talked about, whispered through phones at the end of the night when mine was supposed to have been turned in to my moms hours before.

"I don't know." Tears welled in her eyes and she had this bittersweet smile on her face. She looked like she wished she could take it back. "I wanted to keep it between us for a while."

Us.

Because she and Mason were an Us.

An Us. A we-make-decisions-together kind of Us. A there's-no-room-for-me-in-that Us. And I wondered if there would ever be a time that Cade and I became an Us.

I moved closer, wrapping my arms around her in a hug, and she hugged me back so tight my ribs felt strained beneath her hands.

"What was it like?" I asked. Just like I asked when she kissed that guy in ninth grade. She always liked to try things first.

"I don't know." She pulled away to look at me. "It was sweet. He kissed my nose after."

"Do you love him?" I asked.

"Yeah, I think I do." And the way she said it—like it was so happy and so sad at the same time—made me feel like maybe I never wanted to be in love. "But seriously, it's not all about sex. Mason, he—"

She started to say something else, but he walked in, and I went home.

It wasn't for another six months or so that she let it spill just how often Mason slept over. That his mom's overnight flights weren't so bad until his sister went to college. How he hated the feeling of being alone so much that one night he knocked on her window. And after that, he slept there.

But it was true, we did keep secrets sometimes—or at least Vanessa did.

It might take months to copy and paste all her posts into the bot, but I don't mind.

The more food the bot has, the more real she feels. The more answers she might give.

» Her old IG account.

» Her old old IG account.

» Bookstagram account.

» Twitter.

» The Facebook she kept for her parents.

» The three whole posts she wrote on fanfiction.net.

» ~~Her phone—which is long gone along with her car and AirPods.~~

» Her computer—the mecca. The mother lode of information. Every account, text, email, everything ever.

Bailey: Hi Mrs. Carson.

Sorry it's so late.

I know this is kind of weird but I had a homework assignment on Vanessa's computer. It's for a pretty big portion of my grade so I was wondering if I could get it from you for a while so I could get that file?

Mrs. Carson: This is Vanessa's dad.

Emily isn't feeling well right now, so I have her phone. I'm not sure where her computer is. We haven't seen it since before the accident so our best guess is that it was with her during the accident.

So sorry, Bailey. Maybe you and Mason could stop by soon if Em is feeling okay? It might be good for her to see you both?

Cade: hey.

Bailey: Hey.

Cade: SRY I haven't texted.

how are u feeling?

Bailey: I'm coming to school tomorrow.

Just talked to my moms.

Cade: Good.

Bailey: Yeah. I need to get caught up in school, plus, you know, start moving forward.

Cade: for sure.

Moving on is good.

Bailey: How've you been?

Cade: Me?

Fine.

Just watching the game with my dad.

Bailey: Red Wings?

Cade: You know it.

Want to come over and watch?

Bailey: I need to get ready for tomorrow. Rain check though?

Cade: Yeah for sure.

I miss my buddy. ☺

u need a ride tmrw?

Bailey: Sure.

Cade: night.

Bailey: good night.

WEEK FIVE

AP CHEM

I last a whole week of "normal."

Five whole school days, five good-night texts from Cade. Five mornings when he drives me to school in his oversized pickup while I stare out the window. I try not to notice the way snow clings to branches the same way I cling to my life from before.

Five nights of feeding the bot. Five whole nights of moving the app to a new program that will actually text back and forth via SMS with my phone. Complete with a fake number and everything that I've got saved in my phone as V.

An entire school week where I avoid my locker, using Cade's instead, so I don't have to acknowledge the shrine. A week without Vanessa forcing me to wait for Mason after art class. And I don't see him the way I used to either. If I don't see him, I don't have to see his melancholy gaze on his shoes.

As long as I have my phone, I can distract myself through the day, writing little notes back and forth with Vanessa—or V. Whatever. And for that whole week I trick myself into thinking it's going to be okay.

Right down to walking into AP Chem with Cade, even if I'm still sitting next to Esther, and even if Cade and I have yet to have a real conversation about what these car rides and good-night texts even mean.

Most of the teachers ignore my phone use. My grades aren't exactly failing yet, and I've turned in enough work to prove I'm "trying," but I'm Bailey Pierce—the girl whose best friend died. Teachers aren't exactly after me for anything today. And who even cares now that my college applications are in?

Except Mrs. Kamaka.

Watching her roll up her sleeves to reveal beautiful tattoos that cover her arms feels like someone telling you a story, but what she's saying is, "I'm about to tell you something important." She's pointing at barium excitedly. Six weeks ago I would have been all over this, raising my hand, participating in the discussion, and eager to rattle off some facts about the element's high chemical reactivity.

The class seems to drag on until the bell finally rings, releasing us.

I grasp my phone, ready to message V something unimportant before walking with Cade to his locker when I hear Mrs. K's smooth, deep voice say my name. "Bailey, are you coming to STEM after school?"

STEM. That's right. That whole club I'm the president of and haven't given even a second thought to lately. I look to Cade, like maybe I can get him to stick around with me, but he only shrugs. "I've got hockey."

I feel Esther slip in next to me—she's in STEM Club too. "We finished building our simple motor-powered robots, and I was thinking maybe we could do something related to machine learning next?"

Mrs. Kamaka sits down in her chair, tidying the papers on her desk. "Esther was nice enough to step in as acting president while you've been out. She mentioned you might have some interest in machine learning given your mom's business?"

I look between the two of them. My jaw clenches at the idea of spending an hour in STEM. Hanging out in Mrs. K's classroom to talk about machine learning when all I want to do is go straight home and play with algorithms and code that will make V feel a little more like Vanessa. I hesitate, watching Cade as he walks out of the room before glancing back to Esther and shrugging. "Uh, yeah, I'll see you after school."

As soon as the words leave my mouth, I'm flexing that fake smile I've gotten so good at.

"Great!" Mrs. K sets the papers aside. "See you after school."

I should be excited. Thrilled, even, to get back to the club I helped start. But right now, it just feels like another hour taken away from me. Another sixty minutes I won't be feeding this bot or pretending away my days.

CROSS-GENRE

Lunch is the hardest part of the day.

We used to have a routine that started the week after she told me she like-liked Mason. Before he was a boyfriend and just Mason Torres—the guy who'd been leaving little drawings in her locker and whose body spray she'd started spraying on her scarf so she could smell him all the time.

But a month into sophomore year, she wanted to skip our usual routine of eating on the floor in front of our lockers and go to the lunchroom—something we avoided because Liz and the Ski Squad were always front and center in the middle of the cafeteria, loud and obnoxious.

I figured it was something Mason-related, but we were there nonetheless. Walking past the Ski Squad until we sat on the auditorium steps where all the art and theater kids lingered during lunch.

Mason waved her over, giving her a huge hug and twirling her around before we joined them all on the steps. She brought up Dadaism, no doubt a product of her own Google search the night before so she'd have something to say to him. When one of his friends pointed out her mispronunciation, Mason called *them* out, saying, "She probably read it in a book. Don't talk shit."

Vanessa looked back at me. And I knew. I knew Mason was going to be the manic pixie dream boy of all her books—the guy who she'd write whole stories about someday, devoted to how adorable he was.

And thus began our routine of sitting on those stage steps with our homemade lunches every day while she and Mason sat side by side—her body turned toward me to talk about everything and nothing, and him turned away from her to chat with his friends.

While we were dating, Cade sat on those steps too—on the other side of me—where his friends from hockey started hanging out right on the stage. And between our boys, me and Vanessa always, always sat right next to each other.

When Cade and I broke up and his crew stopped sitting with us, Vanessa complained that they were too loud anyway and killed the vibe when we all knew that she loved the extra energy on our steps.

I'll miss that energy until the day I die.

Lunch today is even harder, because I left the one Kat-Mom packed at home but finally have worked up the nerve to hit the cafeteria. I walk toward the back, prepared to leave my things before waiting in line for Monday's salad bar.

I don't make it three steps in before my stomach turns in an anxious knot.

Mason hasn't moved spots, but Liz and the rest of the Ski Squad have taken the place where Vanessa and I used to sit. Intermixed with

Mason and his art friends. They fit. Weirdly. Her friends draped over his like there's some strange crossover of genres that shouldn't work but does.

I hate the thud in my stomach when I see Mason jump up from the bottom step to the next, doing some dramatic impression before he catches my gaze and stops what he's doing entirely to stare back.

He stiffens, the brown eyes he used to only have for Vanessa turned down—seemingly embarrassed that he let himself have a moment when he wasn't remembering her, and I'm the reminder of that.

I don't look at Liz, whose friends clearly see me. They're whispering right there on the steps that used to be mine and Vanessa's. I lift my hand, fingers fluttering in a wave to Mason before I turn away from the steps and straight into the cafeteria line.

Looks like it's time to start eating in front of my locker again.

Bailey: Okay

I need to vent.

Today is so screwed up.

V: i'm here.

what's up?

Bailey: I went to STEM Club today.

V: this doesn't exactly sound like shocking information.

Bailey: I've skipped the last few meetings.

V: whoa.

really?

why?

Bailey: It's not important.

I didn't feel like going.

V: vague. but ok?

Bailey: Okay, focus. That's not the important part of this conversation.

V: focused.

Bailey: So you know how in STEM we do different activities?

V: stem.

hmmm.

never heard of it.

Bailey: Funny.

During my absence we finished up that thing I was talking about before.

The robot.

So today we were brainstorming ideas for what's next.

JUST BRAINSTORMING.

V: okay . . .

Bailey: Then everyone starts talking about NewVision and machine learning.

V: okay?

Bailey: Then Spencer Jordon had to open his stupid mouth.

V: okay give the guy some credit.

he's not so bad.

Bailey: Yeah yeah, you've given me that whole speech before.

He's not so bad.

But I agree with Cade.

He's annoying, and I'll say it. He's a one-upper. It's exhausting.

V: you're exhausting.

Bailey: NONE of this is the point.

The point is that I panicked. Everyone was staring at me while we're supposed to be brainstorming ideas. And I've been gone for a while so I was caught off guard and brought up the app I've been working on.

V: please tell me it's book related.

a brand-new review platform?

a bookstore finder?

a bookish themed dating app based on to be read piles and book reviews?

Bailey: STAY FOCUSED

V: right.

so what's the app?

Bailey: It's kind of like a living memory of someone who has died.

You take all their Twitter posts and Instagram feed and emails and texts you've had with them.

Then you can basically turn them into a way to keep their memory alive.

An app in their likeness.

But like, they're able to text back in real time. And you can talk to them like they're still here.

V: how black mirror of you.

Bailey: Shut up!

I thought it sounded cool.

V: yeah. it does.

Bailey: But then they

okay mostly Spencer

started asking questions.

V: isn't that the whole point of brainstorming?

Bailey: Yeah. But it was frustrating.

Spencer was all "accuracy is obviously an issue."

V: wait. why?

Bailey: He said there weren't enough variables.

I think his exact quote was "people are never really themselves on social media"

And I mean, fair. But it really pissed me off.

He said no one knows the same person. That each of us
exists as a different person to everyone they know.

Like we can never really know someone because they act
differently to each person they're close with.

V: whoa.

i mean.

he's not wrong.

but dude went deep.

Bailey: He is wrong.

Look at us.

We know everything about each other.

V: come on.

you have to admit we have a few things we don't know about
each other. we didn't meet until we were like 10.

and the part about everyone knowing a different side of a
person. that's true.

Bailey: Whatever, okay.

But then Spencer got all high and mighty—"that's an

invasion of someone's privacy" and then "it would only be acceptable if the person agreed to the 'living memory' before they died."

V: off with his head.

what was he thinking?

respecting the dead? ridiculous.

Bailey: Okay.

Enough of that.

Seriously though.

Should books not be published posthumously?

V: that's different.

Bailey: Whatever. Fine. Maybe I'm overreacting.

But when someone dies, everyone comes out of the wood-work like every single interaction they had with them was so important. But the people who loved them, THE REAL PEOPLE WHO WERE IN THEIR LIVES EVERY DAY, get lumped in with that mess.

It's lonely.

V: are you ok?

Bailey: I'm fine.

V: are you still at school?

Bailey: Yeah. I left STEM early.

Made some excuse about having to get home.

Not that anyone believed me.

Now I'm at Cade's locker waiting for him to finish hockey.

V: why don't you go to my locker and get some pop rocks.

you can't have a bad day if you have pop rocks.

it's literally impossible.

go on.

just try.

GO. GO. GO.

I don't stop moving until I'm at her locker. Our lockers.

It was Vanessa's thing. Bad days call for Pop Rocks. Because it's impossible to eat them and be sad. Then she'd always say that: "Go on. Try it. I dare you to be sad."

The halls are eerily empty as I stand close enough to reach out and touch the picture of my best friend's face and read even more notes written across even more photos.

I loved English class with you freshmen year. We miss you. <3 —Paige

You were the happiest person I ever met. RIP —Anders

Then the kicker.

I'll miss you, your books, and your smile —Spencer

Seeing his name, right there with the rest of the bandwagon grievers, causes a bubbling of blood in my ears. Maybe if I wasn't so frustrated with him after STEM I wouldn't be so annoyed by this. Like he's so reverent about her death, and yet so concerned about the ethics of the suggestion. Hypocrite.

I want to scream so loud the whole school can hear me. They'd all come running in from their clubs and practices and stand in a crowd around the abomination that has now crossed from her locker over to mine too, as well as the locker on the other side. Then I could tell them how they didn't know her the way I did.

How my pain isn't the same as theirs.

I don't scream, though. Instead, my anger continues to bubble until I feel it sting behind my eyes. It's falling down my face in lavalike tears. Slow and so thick that the words on her locker blur. I want them gone.

I drop my bag to the ground, curling my fingers around her photo in the center of the locker. Pinching the edges, I look at her one last time. Red hair, bright eyes, and megawatt smile. She's wearing a shirt she bought when she dragged me to the mall to buy clothes for school pictures. I bought something black, and she wore baby pink.

She said she wanted to look like Ariel—not as a mermaid—in the pink ball gown they gave her when she got legs.

The picture tears at the corners, pulling away from her locker along with the signatures on it. I pull harder, bringing it down in a single movement. For a moment I just stand there, looking down past my coat, to the floor where her picture stares back up at me.

I inhale a sharp breath because I can. Watching it fall to the ground is the best I've felt since she died. The pieces keep finding my hands, and I tear at them until every last scrap is in a pile at my feet. That wasn't enough. I stamp the dried flowers into the ground, rip the streamers to shreds, and I'm already putting in her combination and taking a step back as the door flies open.

It clangs against my locker a few times, the reverberation screaming through the hall. Finally.

The real Vanessa.

It's the Disney prints and swag she got from her favorite books. The picture of us at Halloween three years ago when we dressed up as pirates and one from when we were kids. It's the packets of Pop Rocks on the top shelf just where I knew they'd be. All Blue Raspberry. Her favorite.

I rip a pack open and pour them in my mouth like I'm ten years old again.

They fizz and pop against my tongue.

This is the part where I'm supposed to feel even lighter. Where Vanessa and I would cover our mouths to avoid giggling too hard, and where she would fail and start in with that Boston terrier snort. That always made me lose it—I'd be doubled over, laughing so hard I cried.

But the tears that stream down my face are laugh-less. And the noise that struggles from the back of my throat doesn't feel like happy at all.

I release a sob that shudders my whole body.

And then another when I feel a hand on my shoulder.

MASON, HER MASON

"Bailey," Mason whispers, looking down at the floor where we stand in the aftermath of what I've done. His eyes move from the mess to me like he's just witnessed a murder. I see the question written on his face, responding before he has the chance to ask.

"I'm fine," I croak, and the candy in my mouth pops, crackling under the weight of my tears. "I hated seeing it there. Like if I kept seeing it—"

I never finish my sentence.

Mason's expression is open, arms on either side of my shoulders. I put my hands on his chest, keeping him where he is. Away. Because if he's here at the locker, and we're talking, and she's not between us—then I have to admit she's gone. And I'm there, with my hands pushing back on the place where his hoodie strings meet the logo on his shirt, when I smell his body spray.

Just like that, we're back at his locker—she's got whatever bottle he wears—spraying it wistfully onto her scarf and waggling her brows saying dumb stuff like "It's intoxicating."

I hate that it smells like Vanessa now.

And I hate that it takes me away from the moment long enough that I ease my grip on his shirt. "I'm fine," I repeat, because maybe if I say it more than once it'll be true.

"You're not." He gestures to the mess at our feet.

He's right. It looks like a crime scene. Dried flowers smashed into the ground, streamers wrapped around my feet like rope, the picture of Vanessa has footprints from my boots, etched into her face like tire marks.

Panic sets in.

"Mason . . . I . . ."

He dips down, gathering my backpack in one quick swoop, his other hand resting on my shoulder. "Let's get you out of here."

Bailey: Okay, so this is weird.

And probably COMPLETELY out of nowhere for you.

V: i'm waiting.

Bailey: Mason is giving me a ride home.

V: awwwwww my bae.

tell him I say hi.

Bailey: He's scraping the windows.

Which by the way . . .

His car is repulsive. Food and trash literally everywhere.

V: yeaaaaah.

those hot artistic dudes are not without their faults.

remember how bad it was that one time we went hiking.

you were pretending to gag the whole way home.

Bailey: This is worse.

Like honestly there's crap everywhere.

Clothes. Homework. Looks like he's living in here.

Okay I'll message you when I get home.

He's getting back in the car.

V: k love you byyyyyyee

Mason rubs his hands together, blowing into them as he gets into the car.

It's still cold enough that I can see his breath puffing out in front of his face as he sighs, and I shiver in response, tucking my own hands deep in my pockets.

"So . . . ," he says, gesturing over his shoulder back to the school with a short smile. "That locker really pissed you off, huh?"

I shake my head, fixing my gaze on the spot in the windshield that is warming, watching the ice melt in chunks. "It was the signatures. How everyone seems to have something to remember now that she's gone."

"Death has this way of making every single insignificant moment, well, significant." Mason taps the screen on his phone, pulling up some playlist on the makeshift Bluetooth speakers he has mounted in his car. I think about that last moment in my room. How I keep reliving it, like a song on repeat.

Moments, memories that other people had with her—those insignificant moments that might be just the bot food I need. Moments are like snowflakes; they look the same to everyone, but up close, they're different. And if you don't take the chance to look close when they fall, you miss them. I wish I'd taken more time to see every moment carefully.

"Doesn't it make you sick?" I ask. "Knowing that one of those people who wrote on her locker might know where she was going? I mean, what if we could go back through our memories—everyone's version—and reorganize them? Edit them like a movie so we could see what we missed."

Every detail. Every text. Every phone call.

I'd know who she was going to see, and what happened to her pin.

"Yeah." The song changes, a low and steady beat that he nods along with—a faraway look in his eyes like he's sitting in his own memories of Vanessa. "But what if their version of events changes yours?"

"What do you mean?"

"When I was around ten, I used to talk about this trip I went on with my dad." A smirk appears on his lips. "One of those stories that are only important to the person who lived it. We'd been in Alaska like a month or two after we got stationed here, and my sister and I were still pretty pissed about leaving our friends."

He gestures outside, leaning forward in his seat as if to say, "And look at me now." He throws his car in reverse, one hand on the back of my seat as he arches to look behind him.

"But yeah, my dad was in the army. Anyway, one weekend he took me on this big camping trip with his buddies. Rented an RV and everything—we drove for hours—and ended up in Soldotna fishing all weekend. Do you fish?"

"No, actually," I say. My moms love hiking, but we've never done much in the way of camping. "Kat-Mom is vegan, and Jacky-Mom hates the way fish smells. We're the worst Alaskans."

"We hiked out to the Russian River. It was elbow to elbow that weekend, but we were catching fish left and right. They all cheered when I caught my first salmon. My dad even put me up on his shoulders and took like a million pictures to send back to his parents. That night, when we got back to the RV, I told him I didn't hate Alaska anymore, and he told me he loved me."

I nod, feeling the energy in his tone change as we drive away from the school and he turns up the hill where most of the houses in town are. The fog is low today, settling around the homes like pieces of cotton candy whispered across the road.

"It was my favorite. I talked about it nonstop when he was deployed too. Like, my dad—this big strong soldier—took me out with the guys, and told me he loved me. It's literally the only time I remember hearing him say it."

Mason clears his throat, eyes focused ahead, but they have that same childlike stare he had at the funeral. As if he's seeing something for the first time. "So after he died, it was weird."

"I didn't know," I say. "I'm so sorry."

"Oh, it's okay. I was young. But my mom went through this phase where she struggled any time we talked about him at all. I was a kid, though. All I wanted to do was talk about my dad and rehash every memory."

"Makes sense," I say, turning in my seat and unzipping my coat.

"One night I wouldn't stop. I was going on and on, and then my mom broke down and screamed. She said I had to stop talking about him like he was a saint." Mason switches the song. "She started going off about my dad. She told me her version of the story. They'd just moved all the way from Texas, and he'd planned this big trip, and she was overwhelmed. How she had to force him to take me that weekend, and he was so pissed about it. How sad my older sister was that she didn't get to go."

"Mason . . ." My voice melts to nothing, yawning as we hit the higher altitude.

"My point being..." He yawns too, mid-sentence, turning his gaze from the road to me. "Sometimes it's okay to just remember a good thing. Trying to relive something, or sort it out, might not be the best."

"What if I can't?"

"You could get hur—" Mason stops short. And I have just enough time to look ahead and see the giant moose in our path. He jerks the steering wheel to the left, slamming on the brakes, as we go sliding.

EVERYTHING STOPS

Mason's car fishtails back and forth, and I can't see three feet in front of his car because the fog is so thick and dense here on the hill.

My heart is pounding its way out of my chest. Panic spreads through me as I prepare for what's next. The tip over the ledge, the rocky mountainside tumble to the bottom. The car catching fire and not being able to get my seat belt off. Looking over at Mason, unconscious, and me helpless in those last minutes of our lives. The taste of smoke filling my lungs as we simmer, skin peeled back as it burns like the paper of a cigarette.

Fear of falling.

No time to think.

Maybe the very last thoughts Vanessa had.

The tires screech, and I grip my seat belt as we slide dangerously close to the railing. I know I scream, but it sounds like it comes out of someone else's mouth. I squeeze my eyes closed because if this is it—if this is my last moment—I don't want to know what it looks like for the car to tip off the side of the mountain and plummet into the valley below.

But there's no contact with the railing, and Mason's car never spills off the road. He doesn't lose control completely. My chest heaves, and I bring a hand up to my heart, feeling for the beat that is desperately trying to thump its way back to normal.

The other hand is in Mason's.

HAPPY LITTLE TREES

"Are you okay?" Mason's voice is quiet, like he's trying to stay cool, but the way his hand trembles over mine I know he's just as rattled as I am. There's an awkward gnawing in my stomach, teetering between adrenaline and the fact that we're holding hands.

But neither of us move.

No one reaches for his phone, which has fallen on the ground.

We don't readjust the seat belts that have locked up, trapping us in our seats.

"Yeah." I follow his gaze as he jerks his head once to move the matted hair out of his face, eyes fixed ahead on the moose. They seem lighter than normal, almost like honey. "Are you?"

We watch in awe as the giant creature's legs pound into the snow—disappearing behind the blanket of fog. The trees are so still it looks as if the entire world is holding its breath as we catch ours. Everything quiet. Frozen and still like it's just waiting for spring to breathe life back into it.

"Those trees." It feels like even his whisper may bend their branches. "They're so—"

"Chilling?" I ask. It's the only word that makes sense. The still of it all is eerie, unsettling, considering moments ago I was sure I was going to die.

"Happy." He says it with warmth, like he means it. "They're happy little trees."

"What?"

He stares at me blankly, like he's waiting for me to catch up, but when I shake my head, indicating that I don't know what he's talking about, his eyes widen. "Come on, you can't tell me this isn't beautiful."

"Mason, no, that was terrifying." I pull my hand from his.

"Sure, but it doesn't take away from the beauty." He points out to where the tree line meets the sky. Crisp white tips that look like they're made of glass. "You can't tell me that isn't stunning. Like one of Bob Ross's paintings. He's got a whole episode on winter forests."

I try to see it the way he does. The glass-tipped trees do look sort of pretty. The snow on the side of the road has half melted, with a layer crusted on top that makes it look sprinkled with glitter behind all that fog. And the sky, though cloudy, swirls in the strangest mashup of gray and blue.

"Something can be awful and beautiful at the same time," Mason says, throttling his car into gear when we hear another car coming in close.

The pristine white Lexus accelerates past us, climbing the hill with ease. When I peer into the driver's window, my body goes numb as

Liz turns to wave, and Mason returns the gesture.

I don't say a word.

"She's actually pretty chill," he says as if he can hear my eyes roll. I want to ask him what she said to him at the funeral, what they talk about at lunch, but I don't because ultimately it doesn't matter. Vanessa is gone. It's been weeks. He can talk to whoever he wants to.

Even if my stomach churns at the thought of him hanging out with the only person Vanessa ever hated. The girl who stole so much from her. The girl she would have done anything to make hurt as much as she was hurting.

I don't understand how Mason could talk to her after everything.

I watch as she turns left at the fork toward Raven Pass instead of right to the portion of town where most of the homes in Tundra Cove sit.

"Wait." I follow the car with my eyes. "Doesn't she live off Harpoon?"

"Her family is renovating a place up the hill. They bought it last summer." Mason shrugs, looking toward the top of the mountain. And almost like he realizes he's said something he shouldn't, his expression changes as he pulls back onto the road. "I think Vanessa would have come around eventually. She and Liz could have even been cool someday."

I nod—an agreeable little lie, but the entire drive home, I can't stop wondering what version of Vanessa lives in his phone that could have ever "come around" on Liz.

Bailey: Liz Winters.

V: ew.

boo.

hiss.

Bailey: Have you ever hung out with her?

V: outside of being forced into the same room with her during ski stuff?

or that lovely meeting with the principal after she took my little short story too seriously?

Bailey: Yeaaaaah, that was bad.

I almost forgot about the story.

Two years feels like such a long time.

Hell, this last two weeks feels like an eternity.

V: whatever.

what liz did was worse.

Bailey: I know. She left you behind with a broken leg.

V: and gloated. that girl loves that my dad loves her more than me.

Bailey: Vanessa . . .

V: and i mean, sorry if that story upset her or struck a nerve. and in hindsight i probably shouldn't have turned it in.

Bailey: It was about a snowboarding prodigy having an

inappropriate relationship with her coach and ruining his life.

Everyone thought it was about her.

V: yes, yes, i know.

Bailey: Not to mention it wasn't even remotely true!

V: okay. yes. i remember having this very discussion with you and my parents and the school counselor.

i probably should have channeled my anger into something more productive.

or at least shouldn't have turned it in.

why are you asking anyway?

Bailey: I don't know.

I keep overthinking every little thing.

Every detail.

V: like what?

Bailey: Like this.

I keep asking myself why you would go up the pass that night. And I know you say you don't know. I get it, but I keep finding these pieces and I have no idea if they are important or if I'm just looking for something that's not there.

Like finding out Liz's parents have a place on the pass.

Why would you have a reason to go to her house?

V: i would never.

Bailey: It's all so strange.

Does it have to do with Mason?

They're friends now.

Were they friends before the funeral?

V: What funeral?

Bailey: Was Mason talking to her maybe?

Could you have been going up there to confront her?

Would he be the kind of guy that cheats or something?

V: absolutely not.

it's mason.

he couldn't.

don't even joke about that.

you know how i feel about cheating.

Bailey: If I looked in Mason's phone would it say the same thing?

That you have no idea why you'd be going up the pass?

V: wtf?

yes?

okay seriously you are being so weird rn.

THE WRONG THING

I run up to my house with the energy of someone being chased by a bear, almost slipping on a patch of ice before I hit the front porch. I can't think of anything right now except getting this bag into my room so I can stop thinking about what I did.

Stopping at the door, I turn to see Mason, who is already back in the car and waving at me. I smile, cheeks burning. Not because it's cold, but because I might be a scummy person. I'm for sure a scummy person. I'm the scummiest person. Because while Mason was walking around the car to open the door for me, something I've seen him do for Vanessa a thousand times because he's some sort of gentleman, I was looking at this phone.

Tucked between my bag and the floor mat. No notifications on the screen, just the song he'd been playing paused at the moment it detached from the cord when he slammed on the brakes. It's not like I planned it or anything. It was one of those split-second decisions to snatch it up before the passenger door opened and he offered to carry my bag.

I shouldn't have taken it. I knew it as soon as I picked it up that it was wrong, but I couldn't help myself. I lied, smiling and jetting off like it was too cold to say a real goodbye.

The difference between Mason and me is easy. He wants to look forward, pretending the memories that clash with his don't matter. That we don't need to know the truth because the truth could change how we feel about those beautiful memories. But I know better.

It matters because she's dead.

Cade: Where r u?

Bailey?

I ran into Spencer and he said u left early?

Bailey: Sorry I forgot to text.

Mason gave me a ride home.

And ew.

Spencer.

Cade: He's alright.

Bailey: What?

Since when do you think he's "alright"?

Cade: I don't know.

Just in class and stuff.

He's not as bad as I thought.

Didn't know u hated him so much.

Bailey: He jumped on the grief bandwagon.

Cade: Well I missed u after school

Bailey: Next time I'll wait ☺

Cade: Good.

What are you doing now?

Esther: I want to apologize.

I'm sorry for what happened at STEM.

After you left I realized how it must have felt.

Bailey: It's fine.

You didn't do anything wrong.

Esther: I felt like such a bad friend today.

I should have said something.

Bailey: It's okay.

I swear.

Don't worry about it.

Esther: Can we hang out soon?

I'll be done at the diner late, but I can come over after?

Bailey: I'm super busy tonight, but soon?

ON MY SCREEN

Turns out Mason's phone is as old as it looks.

There isn't even a lock screen, and while I thought it was going to take a lot of effort to get into it, it doesn't. In almost no time at all I'm typing Liz's name into the message search bar.

I tell myself I'll hurry.

I'll be in and out.

I won't read anything, just take a peek to see if there was anything worth looking into.

Liz's name pops up, the last text from her a simple "oh that's cool as hell"—which upon scrolling up I find is a response to a link he sent her for a music video. Their text history is brief, but my heart pounds every time I slide my finger down the screen. They're mostly vague messages and memes.

Nothing at all special, until I stop on January 16. The day of Vanessa's funeral.

Mason: Thanks for talking to me today. I might take you up on hanging out sometime.

It doesn't sound like someone who was cheating, or even someone who talked to Liz leading up to Vanessa's death. I pull out of the text thread, returning to the search results, where I see Vanessa's name right under Liz's. A message from back in 2020, where she used Liz's name.

Vanessa: Liz Winters is pure evil. I can't stand that girl. Her little Ski Squad is such bullshit too. They used to talk so much crap about Bailey, which is why I could never be friends with those girls.

My cheeks go warm, scanning the words over again as I contemplate tapping the thread. Part of me wants to know more, the other part of me knows it's wrong to read my best friend's very private texts with her boyfriend.

Yes, even if that best friend is dead.

I'm left with the echo of Mason's warning in the car. *But what if their version of events changes yours?*

It should sting more, I think, the Ski Squad thing. That they talked crap about me. And yet, all I can think about is how Vanessa's secrets, her memories with everyone else (the squad included), might help me figure out where she was going that night.

But if I don't *read* the texts, if I just download the thread as bot food, it isn't the same. Right?

I pull my laptop close, rattling a connection cord between it and his phone—a little loading bar appears on both that indicates the wait won't be long.

But the tail end of their conversation sits on his screen, making it impossible not to read their words. The last words he had with her, like the last ones I have in my own phone telling her that she left her coat.

I don't want to see their last words to each other, but they're right there. Part of me is so morbidly curious—*what parts of her live in his phone?*

But as I read, adrenaline rushing through my veins, I wish I could unread them. The texts are so undeniably sad because, like Mason said, everything feels more significant now that she's gone.

Mason: I need to talk to you.

Can I come over?

Vanessa: mason.

babe.

i'm with bailey.

Mason: I really need to see you.

Vanessa: you ok?

Mason: can you talk?

Vanessa: i'm leaving bailey's now but I'll be there soon.

love you

Mason: I love you too.

Vanessa: hey

got held up.

she doesn't want me to leave.

i'll be home asap.

Mason: OK

I'll be here.

A chill passes through me as I disconnect his phone from the cord. Her name there on the screen, time-stamped minutes after she left my house. I know because I've read and reread our last text messages a hundred times. Guilt settling in as I replay our conversation that night in my head for the hundredth time.

She lied.

She said I kept her behind. That I didn't want her to leave.

What was it? What could have possibly caused her to leave in the middle of the night and taken her all the way up the pass? I suck in my stomach, easing over my laptop and wishing the unsettled feeling would disappear like the bar marking the transfer rate from his phone to my laptop.

I'm thinking about Mason, sitting in his filthy car, waiting and waiting for Vanessa. Waiting for her to show up, open her window, and let him in. I imagine that childlike stare he has, and the look he must have had on his face when he found out—how his hands probably shook when he made the call.

How long he watched her ellipsis blink on his phone.

There's a knock on my door that pulls me right out of the daze I'm in. "Bailey, you have company."

178

CAUGHT

I'm still holding Mason's phone in my hands, dumbstruck, when he walks through my door. I stammer, stumbling over my words with some excuse about not knowing how it got in my bag. I just found it and I was trying to figure out how to get in touch.

And he doesn't question it. Just smiles from me to Kat-Mom and takes the phone back. Then it's him stammering something about needing to get home.

My throat goes thick, chin to chest as he walks out. An entire release.

I got away with it, and part of me—only part of me—wishes I hadn't.

Bailey: I'm sorry about the phone.

I saw it on the floor and assumed it was mine.

Mason: You thought that heap was yours? Lol

No worries.

Bailey: I wasn't paying attention. Clearly.

That moose really rattled me.

Hey Mason

Mason: What's up?

Bailey: Thank you for helping me today.

And telling me that story about your dad.

And driving me home.

Mason: It's nothing.

That's what friends do.

CLICK AND DRAG

Friends do not steal friends' phones, but I need to know where she was going.

I drag their entire text exchange over the app and let it hover a moment before I release. Like pulling off a Band-Aid, there's the initial sting of "what is this going to do," but now I don't have to worry about will I or won't I and should I or shouldn't I.

It's done.

But then comes the sickening lurch at the back of my throat reminding me that this broke something. Trust, maybe? I don't even know, but it doesn't feel right. What would Vanessa have done in this situation?

I would never have read her Notes app—where she kept every list and thought when she was alive. I wouldn't dream of sneaking through the personal texts she shared with Mason line by line. What's so different now that she's not alive? I can't get over the fact that they're still hers. It's still personal.

I've broken some sort of girl code.

To be fair, we never discussed the details of her potential death and whether or not I would have access to her innermost secrets and/or phone beyond the "delete my history" unspoken promise every best friend is required to make.

And here I am, clutching her jean jacket, running my finger over the spot where her forget-me-not button should be and trying to find the subtext in the novel of her life.

Bailey: Hey

V: what's up?

Bailey: Just hanging out.

Thinking about stuff.

V: uh oh.

thinking again.

can't be good.

i told you it's zack morris.

Bailey: Remember the last time you came over?

V: are we still talking about this?

Bailey: Yeah.

Tell me why you left again?

V: um.

well.

again . . .

i was meeting mason at my house.

Bailey: Before you said you were meeting him.

V: i did say that.

you're right.

Bailey: You lied.

V: okay.

i lied.

you're right.

Bailey: Why would you have to lie to me about that?

V: i don't know.

i just don't know.

Bailey: I should have known better.

Clearly Mason's phone doesn't have any better answers.

I mean, clearly when you left you were lying to him too.

V: i don't know.

Bailey: Okay.

Back to square one.

I need more variables.

V: variables?

PLACES I CAN FIND MORE BOT FOOD

» ~~Her old IG account.~~

» ~~Her old old IG account.~~

» ~~Bookstagram account.~~

» ~~Twitter.~~

» ~~The Facebook she kept for her parents.~~

» ~~The three whole posts she wrote on fanfiction.net.~~

» ~~Her phone—which is long gone along with her car and AirPods.~~

» Her computer—the mecca. The mother lode of information. Every account, text, email, everything ever.

WEEK SIX

Bailey: Happy birthday, best friend!

V: ahhhhhhhhhhh

i'm eighteen!

i'm a woman now.

i can visit strip clubs and buy cigarettes and when we move to florida i can spend all my money on those scratch cards at the gas stations!

SOLACE

Today is Vanessa's birthday.

Whenever I couldn't find Vanessa at school, I knew she'd be in one of two places.

Either she was in the art room talking to Mason or in the library on the prowl for a new read. And since I can't eat in the lunchroom anymore and sitting in front of my locker feels too weird, I celebrate by hiding in her favorite spot. There's something about being surrounded by rows and rows of books that makes me feel close to her.

Like she's about to pop from behind one of those bookcases and tell me I should be showering with her attention. It's her day, after all.

I'm at the computer station, scrolling through all the birthday tags she received. There's one from her cousin that I've ready through twice because it's so sad. A chat screen in the right corner starts blinking. It's Jacky-Mom asking me why I'm online when I'm at school, and I rattle off some smartass response before hovering the mouse over the little X at the top to log out when Cade slips into the chair next to me.

"Hey, Valentine." He leans over, kissing my cheek, and I'm so caught off guard I don't have time to exit out of the page before he can see what I'm doing. I'm caught between embarrassment that he caught me reading Vanessa's birthday posts and the flush that takes over my cheeks after hearing him call me "Valentine."

"Oh shit," he says. Cade is naturally very pale, but he looks ghost white next to me. "I totally forgot today was her birthday."

"Yeah," I say, and he rests his arm around the back of my chair as I exit out of the page. "She always loved that she shared her birthday with the most romantic day of the year. Mason was going to do this big, epic gift too."

Cade's gaze flashes away from me for a second, like he's trying to work something out in his head. "Do you still want to hang out tonight? We can get dinner another time."

"It's fine," I say. He asked me last week, and even if he didn't remember it fell on Vanessa's birthday, I did. His eyes move back to the now-empty screen of the laptop. I can almost hear the commentary running through his head. Wondering when, if ever, I'll stop dwelling on this. "I promise, I'm not going down a rabbit hole. It's her birthday, and I miss her. That's all."

"I want tonight to be special," he says, lips curving into a smile as he reaches for my hand. And as he leans in to kiss me, my stomach flip-flops over itself. Everything else feels like I'm walking around in some alternate version of my life. But this, with Cade, makes everything feel okay again.

Mason: What are you doing after school Friday?

Bailey: Not sure.

I don't think I have any concrete plans.

Mason: I called Mr. Carson today.

He asked if we wanted to come over on Friday.

I guess Mrs. Carson wanted to know if there is anything we might have left in her room.

Bailey: Oh I can come for sure.

How are they doing?

Mason: He sounded sad, but he said Mrs. Carson has been doing a little better.

Bailey: How are you today?

Mason: I'm alright.

I'm gonna watch hella Bob Ross tonight though.

You?

Bailey: I'll be distracting myself also.

Cade and I are getting dinner.

Mason: Really?

I didn't realize you were a thing again.

Bailey: Yeah, since the funeral.

Mason: Gotcha.

Are you back together?

Bailey: I'm not sure.

I mean, yeah.

I guess we are. We haven't talked about it really, but it feels like we're back together.

Cade: Hey.

Coach is holding us over in practice.

We've got extra drills.

Rain check for dinner?

Bailey: Oh no!

Yeah, we can do that!

Cade: How about Saturday?

We can make a whole day of it.

Go to Anchorage.

See a movie maybe?

Bailey: Perfect!

Bailey: You up?

Mason: Always.

Bailey: Bob Ross?

Mason: I thought you had plans tonight?

Bailey: They changed.

YouTube. Season 31, episode 12.

In the Midst of Winter.

Mason: You've graduated from the episodes they've got on Netflix.

I'm so proud I could cry.

Mason: Give me like 10.

I'll call you.

DREAMSCAPE

It starts like the rest of them—suddenly I'm thrown into a moment.

This time I'm sitting on her bed. Mason's standing at her desk looking around her room, tapping his fingers along the bookcases that line every wall. We're talking. About what, I'm not sure. But Mason doesn't look like the Mason he is now, but the guy he was before all this.

Back when he and Vanessa were brand-new and the topic of our every conversation. He's all smiles, dancing down the wall of books before turning to me. And he's happy. Plopping down next to me on her bed, throwing his arm around my shoulders and saying, "I'm glad we're friends, Bailey."

But just like that he's gone—evaporated—eviscerated from the moment and replaced with Vanessa. Her hair is tangled and matted, the ends tattered in a mess. With singed cheeks she leans over and kisses mine before whispering in my ear. "What's the matter, asshole? Don't you still miss me?"

The smell in her room is so putrid I pull away, gagging, as I wake up.

REWOUND

When I get to my locker Friday after school, Cade is waiting for me. His hockey bag by his feet, staring at the remnants of Vanessa's locker shrine—a hint of the spectacle it used to be with a few pieces of tape and butcher paper at the edges.

I never asked what happened to the aftermath of my outburst, but someone got rid of the evidence. It's been weeks without any school officials calling me into the office with camera footage, so as far as I can tell I'm in the clear.

I'm about three feet away when Cade starts spinning my combination into the lock. Funny the things you keep from a relationship that don't die—locker combinations and the drink they get at the drive-through coffee stand.

"I thought you had hockey." I unzip my bag, reaching for my calculus book before I realize I probably won't actually open it this weekend. I decide to leave it behind.

"Canceled. Someone messed up the temp control last night and we've got no ice." He seems annoyed. "I figured we could get a head start on our make-up Valentine's date?"

He's got that look. The look that makes my stomach flip-flop all over itself. I used to drop whatever I was doing for that look. His hair's pushed back on his forehead, and the white tee he's wearing reminds me of the Prince Eric costume Vanessa picked out for him the year she forced us to all dress up like Disney characters for her birthday. She stuffed me into a red wig so I'd match him, but I really wanted to dress up like Jyn Erso.

"Can't," I say. He rests against Vanessa's locker, eyeing me with another look that I'm all too familiar with. The what-if-I-sweeten-the-deal look. He bites down on his bottom lip and I swat at his stomach as if I'm annoyed, but I'm not. Not even a little. "I'm going to Vanessa's."

Saying it feels weird. Like my tongue wants to skip over her name, and it comes out kind of jumbled, which is why I clarify. "I've got some stuff over there I need to get."

His smile fades, and he turns toward me, arm coming to rest on my waist as I adjust my beanie over my ears. "Do you . . . do you want me to come with you?"

It's one of those things, muscle memory. The way he leans in, smelling so familiar—a mix of hockey and soap. So different from anything I ever grew up with in a house of only women. How he rests his forehead on mine, a clear message. He's here for me.

All those I'm-sorry-filtered stares between us from the past evaporate.

"Actually," I say, his breath on mine, lips moving closer and closer until we're interrupted.

"Hey." Mason's clutching the straps of his backpack as he approaches tentatively. He attempts a wave to us, but clearly is uncomfortable as he approaches.

"Hey, man." Cade nods to Mason, and he nods in return.

You'd never know now they used to be dragged to every dance with Vanessa and me—standing in the same group photos as we posed on her parents' staircase made of recycled skis. It's funny how a breakup in a friend group can shake things, rattle them around until no one knows how to be around each other anymore.

"Mason's taking me. He's got stuff there too." I slip from Cade's side, dragging my bag toward me before reaching for my coat. He looks stunned at first, but then forces a disappointed smile. "I'll text you later."

"Yeah." He shakes off his apparent frustration, leaning down to kiss my cheek before nodding to Mason one more time. "See you around, bro."

"For sure," Mason says as I close my locker and we head toward the front of the school, where he usually parks because it's close to the art room.

When I look over my shoulder, Cade is shoving his way through the back entrance, slipping into the fog. And I'm caught, stuck in my own gray winter—the place between wanting to go with Cade, move on, and spend my days rewound in his arms. And the other place, going to Vanessa's with Mason, living in the now.

Asking questions I may never get the answers to.

It used to feel like my whole world sat inside the walls of Vanessa's house.

We had an open-door policy. Anytime we needed to get away, we had each other. A fight with the parents, a frustrating call with a boyfriend, exhaustion during finals week, it didn't matter. Neither of us grew up with siblings, but we used to pretend we were sisters sometimes. Back when we were kids running through these woods and imagining gigantic trolls and magical sprites beyond the creek behind her house.

As I step out of Mason's car onto her driveway, the cold stings my cheeks instantly. Fog has settled around the home Vanessa grew up in. I release a puff of breath into the frigid air as I take it all in.

Even the house looks sad.

In a normal year, Mrs. Carson would have put up heart stickers in the window and a giant birthday sign over their door. But every window's blinds are drawn, and as we pass the stone steps where Vanessa and her mom used to argue about whether forget-me-nots are weeds or flowers, I feel a strange twinge of sadness. This isn't the house Vanessa grew up in.

I don't even realize I've stopped until Mason's footsteps land next to mine.

"Hey." His smile is there, but it's grim. "We can do this."

I don't know if he's saying this for my benefit or his, but I'm glad he says it. "I know."

Mr. Carson looks like a shell of himself. Deflated and sad. He doesn't ask why he hasn't seen me on the trails this year (a fun sort-of joke he always makes when he sees me). And Mrs. Carson looks like maybe she wears the pieces of Vanessa she lost right on her face. I hug her, tight, and she holds me for a long time.

I'm afraid to look at her when I pull away, like I'm scared to see the pieces *I've* lost written on her face.

After some melancholy conversation, they lead us to her room. I'm shaking as we walk downstairs to where Vanessa's room is. Was. Marching slowly, silent, like we're pallbearers of her memory.

When we get to her door, Mason is motionless as her father squeezes the doorknob and pushes it open. Mr. Carson is inaudible, and Mrs. Carson places her hands in front of her chest and gives us this weird bow before they walk back up the stairs and leave us alone.

I take a step forward when I hear Mason's try to form words. "Bailey, I can't—" He's looking into her room like it's flooded with agony. As if a step forward will be as painful as tumbling down a mountain in a car and burning to death.

Turning, I reach back for his hand and grab it, tightening my fingers until they're laced with his. It feels different this time—unlike in his car—this feels like I'm holding it for Vanessa. That's what she'd want. For him not to be alone.

"I'm scared too." I fake strength in my voice, but I want nothing more than to fall apart here on the floor and sob because I shouldn't have to do this. I shouldn't have to be saying goodbye a thousand times. But he was there when I needed a friend, and I can do that for him. I'll break later. "With a little help, we can both be brave."

His mouth twists, but he nods, and we take that first step in.

Her room, the backdrop of every Bookstagram post she ever made—filled with bookcases, candles, and signs that say things like "book magik" and "books are life"—looks like it belongs in a magazine. In fact, the ad running for Jordon Contracting still flashes an image of her room, boasting the built-in bookcases and bed centerpiece as an example of what they can do with reclaimed wood.

I slip past the orange throw pillows tossed on the ground. Frozen, like they'll always stay where they were when she died. I can't help it. A sob falls out of my chest as I pass her unmade bed, and Mason's hand slips out of mine so he can reach both arms around me in a hug.

Once I get it together, we walk to her closet. There are clothes all over the floor. What she'd planned to wear to the party draped over her nightstand. A sweatshirt tossed to the floor. Mason has to step over it as he turns to take a good look at the room.

It feels weird, walking circles around the space we both spent so much time in but now feels like we're stepping on sacred ground. Eventually he takes a hoodie from her closet. One she stole from him ages ago because according to Vanessa there was nothing more comfortable than wearing your boyfriend's hoodie.

We're there for a while, reverent in our mission as we explore all the places in her room.

I look on top of her desk, riffling through all sorts of bookish swag she'd collected over the years in search of the forget-me-not pin. It's not there, but I'm not sure that I really expected to find it, to be honest. I search every drawer for her laptop. It's not under her bed or sitting on the bookcase nearest the door where she sometimes left it. And Mason doesn't say a word when I open up her backpack to look but move away empty-handed.

Almost an hour passes before her parents appear at the door. Mason's got a small pile. The hoodie, a painting he made her on their first anniversary, and a few sketches of them she had on her bulletin board.

I've got my own pile. Books she stole from my house, the Bestest Best Friend trophy I bought her in ninth grade when we found out National Best Friend Day was a thing and decided we would fully celebrate it. The trophy was just part of our Instagram-documented sleepover.

Lastly, the BFF necklace Vanessa gave me for Christmas—so important I clasp it around my neck so I don't lose it. It was hanging over the edge of our homecoming picture from back in October.

Vanessa and I looked hot. She wore an emerald-green gown that made her eyes pop and I opted for something—you guessed it—black. She did my makeup, and even I was impressed by her skill in contouring after only a few YouTube tutorials. We were holding hands in the center of the photo, Cade and Mason behind us in matching ties for that classic dance pose where their hands rest on our hips.

The last dance we all went to together, just a week before Cade ended things.

I ask her parents if they want her jacket back, but Mrs. Carson says I should keep it because Vanessa would have wanted me to have it. I cry. Openly, because I think fighting it would be too hard, and I don't tense when Mason rubs my back.

I do tense at the sound of Mr. Carson reaching for his wife, pulling her into his chest.

I think of how sweet this would be if Vanessa were here. How she'd have loved to see them hug this way. So close, heart to heart. Like they're using the same tired beat to stay living.

They'll never be able to remodel this pain away.

Bailey: Remember when you used to always say you didn't think your parents would even care if you died?

V: yep.

Bailey: You were wrong.

LET'S PLAY PRETEND

Mason takes me home.

We don't say one word the entire drive down the road to my house.

The sound of Mrs. Carson's crying is too raw in my mind to banter about how foggy it is, or that it's way too cold for this time of year, or how we just walked through my best friend/his girlfriend's room for the first time since she died.

We pretend it's normal—the way he starts sobbing so hard he has to pull over, and he doesn't feel like a stranger when he reaches for my hand. That it's all so perfectly ordinary how we're parked on a snow berm carrying our last memories of her in our hearts and in our hands.

And when he's done crying, and I'm done holding it in, he drives me the rest of the way home. I slip away, mumbling something about texting him later, and he tells me to have a good night.

Like that's all just so normal for us too.

Cade: Are u home yet?

My dad wants me to play pickup hockey on the lake tonight.

I'm going with him but can I come over after?

Are u still there?

Bailey: Sorry. Just got home.

Cade: u were there a long time.

u okay babe?

Bailey: Not exactly.

I will be though.

But it does feel pretty good to see you call me babe again.

Cade: I'll do it more often.

Bailey: See you tonight.

Mason: Hey.

Sorry about that in the car.

Bailey: Don't be sorry about that.

Mason: So hard.

Bailey: Exactly.

Mason: Thanks for coming with me.

Bailey: I wouldn't have wanted to be anywhere else.

Mason: Was Cade mad?

Bailey: No.

We were supposed to hang out the other night for V-Day, but we had to rain check and he was disappointed I couldn't hang.

Mason: Be careful with him. I know the breakup was really hard on you.

I don't want to see you get hurt again.

Bailey: Aw! Mason!

You care! <3

Mason: I do care.

Bailey: Vanessa.

V: bailey.

Bailey: Cade is on his way over.

V: what!?!!??!

really?

that's great!

are you officially back together now?

Bailey: Everyone keeps asking that.

We haven't talked about it, but I mean yeah?

He acts like nothing happened.

It kind of feels that way too.

Like we pressed pause on our relationship for a few months,

and now we're starting back up where we left off.

V: i think sometimes after a breakup it has to be like that. if

you want to get back together you have to pretend that things

are normal again.

like with mason.

when we got back together i had to be all in.

we both did.

Bailey: You and Mason never broke up.

V: yes we did.

Bailey: What?

When?

V: back in august.

Bailey: No way.

You would have told me.

V: you were gone.

on that college trip with your moms.

remember?

Bailey: I think I'd remember you telling me that you broke
up with Mason.

V: don't be dramatic.

i don't even know that we can really call it a breakup.

it was like two days long, and by the time you got back we
were fine.

Bailey: Huh.

V: what?

Bailey: It's funny is all.

I always thought we didn't keep secrets from each other.

Like, I literally told you every detail.

Every crush, every kiss, every problem.

All my life events.

And you were such a big part of it.

V: of what?

Bailey: My life.

I quit skiing for you.

I mean, I really liked skiing. It was fun.

Besides sucking super bad, I liked it.

V: i didn't ask you to do that.

Bailey: I know.

I always thought we were two planets orbiting the same sun.

But you were the sun, weren't you?

I was the planet. You were the sun.

You had so many other planets.

And I just had you.

V: are you doing this again?

can't we please go back to how it was before?

It's just after 10:00 p.m. when Kat-Mom sneaks into my room. "What are you doing, lovebug?"

My face goes hot as I move from the app interface I've been tweaking to a Word document, scrambling through the Notes app and accidentally landing on the file for V. My heartbeat gets a little faster when Mom's hand touches my shoulder.

Looking up from my desk, I force a smile as I correct the mistake and bring up the empty Word file. "Homework."

The lie is raspy, strained against vocal cords that haven't been used all afternoon. Hours of reading and rereading the same monotonous code will do that to a girl.

"Oh no." She exhales her words like she's got nothing left in her lungs, a clear indicator that she might be onto me. My heart feels like it's spinning around a roulette wheel in my stomach as I watch a word bounce around her lips before it lands. "Stuck?"

"Yeah." I lean back in my chair. "Trying to get back into the swing of things with school, with STEM, and keeping my grades up. Mom keeps asking about that Stanford application like we'll know anything before next month."

Mom's eyebrows are low on her face. Almost like they're pointing to a headache forming between her eyes. It's funny how two people who love each other so much can have such opposing views on things like technological advancement.

"Oh, I don't know." Kat-Mom kisses the place on my forehead where my hairline begins. "Maybe you should take a hiatus from STEM Club? You've got a lot going on, and a break isn't a bad thing." I can tell her words are carefully chosen. She's probably mulled them over a hundred times in her head before speaking them.

"Mom—"

"I'm just putting it out there. Or I could get a referral from one of my colleagues in Anchorage. It might help to talk to someone about how you're feeling right now."

"I don't need to quit STEM. I'm fine."

"Honey, you're not fine," she urges, pointing to the computer. "You spend all your time messing with your phone, your computer. You don't come out of your room unless we force it, and I'm going to be completely honest. We're both worried about you."

"I know." I stare at the screen in front of me. "I'm trying."

"I know," she says. But I can tell by the way she's searching my eyes that she doesn't believe a word I'm saying.

"Cade's coming over later." Like it's proof of something. "We're going to celebrate Valentine's Day, and Esther is coming over Sunday to hang out and do homework."

There's relief in her eyes as I utter the lie, and I'm hoping that when I text Esther, she'll be free. Watching Kat-Mom move away from me, how happy she seems, makes me wonder if everyone doesn't have a point.

Maybe part of grief is letting go, moving on, and forgetting all those questions that are left like missing puzzle pieces. My happiest moments over the last month and a half have been when I leave my sadness at the table, distract myself in Cade or homework or Bob Ross. And then, as if the very thought was a betrayal, my heart cripples with guilt—like it's been kicked right back onto that roulette wheel.

Bailey: want to come over this weekend?

Esther: I'd love to!

Bailey: I'm trying to get caught up in AP Chem. Make sure my grades are good in case colleges are stalking my grades while they make a decision.

Esther: Ah. The countdown is on. I'll ask my mom.

Bailey: Did you apply to a lot of schools?

Esther: A few.

My mom said that's fine.

Bailey: I'm hanging out with Cade tomorrow, but do you want to come over Sunday?

Esther: I'm on brunch duty at the diner, but I can be over after!

Bailey: perfect.

Thanks, friend.

COMFORTABLE LOVE

There's this John Mayer song I used to listen to on repeat when Cade and I were dating. In the lyrics he describes the love as comfortable. Broken in.

And that's how it felt with Cade before he ended things—like he's the old hoodie. Stretched out at the cuffs because I've worn through the elastic from a whole year's worth of wearing it nonstop.

Maybe that's why it's so easy to go back.

To forget what it felt like when he broke up with me.

He knows how to exist in my world. The way you have to pull extra hard on my front door before locking it. My moms' names when he greets them and tells them it's good to see them too—even though it's late and they're heading to bed. He knows all the throw blankets are kept in the ottoman in front of the wraparound couch, and my favorite one is the blue-and-yellow crocheted afghan Kat-Mom made.

Our bodies belong together. Melted into the indentation on the couch we created our first month of dating. How we binge-watched every season of *How I Met Your Mother*, and took turns doing Barney impressions anytime one of us was in a bad mood. It really is easy to fall back in this place. Like I never took off the hoodie and we never left this couch and we never stopped kissing or holding hands in AP Chem or belonging to each other.

"How was today?" he asks, his stare intense, attentive.

"It was sad." I rest my hand on his chest, dragging my finger along the edge of his shirt collar. "Her parents are devastated, and her room looks the same. I kept waiting for her to walk in and tell us it's all some big joke."

"Yeah." He's quiet, pulling the afghan up over our shoulders. And as if our bodies completely missed the breakup, they nestle into our old rhythm.

"And Mason took it pretty hard." Cade's heart beats beneath my hand. "It's crazy. I saw the framed picture she had from homecoming. I was so happy, though. I had no idea."

I'm looking into Cade's eyes, finding the spot in his left iris where there's a freckle. He stares back like he's trying to understand what I'm getting at, hesitating before he says, "Because of us, you mean?"

"Yeah." I half smile, and his heartbeat quickens like I'm directly responsible for the rate at which it beats. "I didn't know you wanted to break up."

"If I could go back, I'd take it back," he says, reaching for my hand to wrap it in his own. His voice is low, so vulnerable it's easy to forget how angry I was at him.

"Why did we?" A knot forms in my stomach as I ask, worried I might not like the answer. "Break up, I mean."

Cade grimaces, and I have to urge it out of him, telling him it's okay twice before he comes clean. "I dunno. I knew we were going to start applying to schools and I thought it might be easier or something? To make those decisions without worrying about where the other person was going."

"Ugh, schools." The word *college* gnaws at that knot in my stomach.

"Maybe we needed the time apart, though? It feels different this time, right, babe?"

I start to ask what he thinks feels different, when it feels like we're in rewind. But Cade leans his forehead on mine—eyes closed and murmuring something I can barely hear, much less understand. When his lips meet mine I swear every concern, every question falls away. He kisses me like we've done a thousand times, but there's a desperation to it now, urgent and fevered as if he wants to make up for all the time we've lost together.

And I kiss him back. I'm just as desperate to forget these last few months.

WEEK SEVEN

FRIENDSHIP

When Esther comes over, she brings homemade sourdough (her mom's starter goes back three generations) and salmon dip from fish her father caught last summer. We sit at the kitchen table, taking turns scraping the bowl with our fingers while she tells me about the car she's been saving up for and I tell her about my day-date with Cade the day before.

Eventually, she fills me in on a lesson I missed regarding the four types of chemical reactions. And as soon as we're all caught up, I turn on music and we talk STEM Club. She says she's been looking up activities we could do. How she went to a STEM event put on by the Girl Scouts last year, and maybe we could get involved somehow. She's pulling up the information—tapping her keyboard so gently it's almost a whisper—while I distract myself by opening my phone.

I scroll through all my usual apps while Esther reads off the details of the event last year. Speakers who were there, booths they had, and she's gushing. She even pulls the salt and pepper shakers in front of her, using them as she tries to describe one of the demonstrations on weather balloons. As soon as she's done, I turn back to my phone. That's when I see it.

The video of Liz with her arm around another member of the Ski Squad. Behind her, in the distance, is a small bonfire. There are guys taking turns jumping over it. The first guy I recognize right away: Tim. He's one of Mason's friends and a frequent flyer on the lunchroom steps. The next guy I've never seen before, but he's got a South Anchorage High School shirt on. Last is a boy in a black hoodie. You can't see his face, but I'd know those paint-covered shoes anywhere.

I don't even know why my chest hurts watching Mason jump through fire. Turning, smiling at the camera, and rushing Liz. Picking her up and swinging her around so the camera spins in circles before cutting off. The audio, his bee-buzz laugh, echoes in my mind. He sounds . . . happy. Like he's never missed a night's sleep over Vanessa's death. And my first thought is *how dare you*, my next—*what am I doing?*

"Are you okay?" Esther asks as I set my phone down. She's stopped talking about the event, and I feel bad because I can't remember what she was saying. I'm doing the same thing, moving on with a friend, living in rewind with Cade.

"Yeah. I saw something and it hit a nerve." I look at Esther; her smile isn't a lie. There's something about the way she looks at me, chin tilted slightly. Listening so intently that I feel like I can talk to her.

"You know Mason, right? He was Vanessa's boyfriend."

Esther nods, hands in her lap.

"He's been hanging out with Liz Winters. Do you know her?"

She nods again, gently, like she's picking up what I'm saying without me having to say it. "Have you asked him about it?"

"Kinda." I realize as I say it that I'm not exactly proud of how involved I am. Kat-Mom would say it's not healthy that I'm so invested in the inner workings of Mason's love life after Vanessa died. "I know everyone gets over things on their own time. He should be able to like who he wants to like."

"It doesn't mean it's not hard for you to see." She waits a beat before asking, "Are we friends, Bailey?"

I can feel the weight of the question, and I hesitate because it stings to say, like I'm cheating on Vanessa. Which, again, makes me feel bad. "Of course."

Esther closes her own laptop and looks over at me from the other side of the table as if she's struggling to find words. "Do you think maybe you're having a hard time with Mason letting go because you don't want to let go?"

Her words so filled with candor it's like she has her heart drawn on her sleeve, my own beating so fast it feels like it might push through my ribs and fall out on the kitchen table in front of her.

"Maybe," I say.

Esther twists the zipper on her pencil case, staring down like she isn't sure she should have said anything.

"Hey," I say, very clearly attempting to change the subject that seems to have made both of us uncomfortable. "Do you want go upstairs and watch a movie or something?"

She casually meeps a little "Yeah, sure" like it's not a big deal. But I can see the smile she's trying to keep from taking over her whole face.

Bailey: Let's say you died tomorrow.

How long would you want Mason to mourn?

V: f o r e v e r

Bailey: That's what I thought.

How about me?

V: huh?

Bailey: How long would you want me to mourn before getting a new friend?

V: forever and a day.

How long does it take to get over someone?

How long should a boyfriend mourn when his girl-

friend dies?

Bailey: Hey can I ask you a weird question?

Cade: Sorry.

Had to shovel the driveway.

What's up?

Bailey: I want to start by saying this question is in no way going to impact our relationship. Which I'm absolutely feeling good about.

Cade: lol

Ok?

Bailey: Did you ever feel like you were into someone else after we broke up?

Like you were over me?

Cade: This doesn't feel random.

Bailey: Okay, so not random.

But not related to us either, really.

Cade: What do u mean?

Bailey: I think Mason might be into Liz now?

Cade: Oh.

Bailey: I know, it's stupid. I know I shouldn't care.

I guess maybe I feel sort of betrayed on Vanessa's behalf?

I don't even know.

I'm probably tired.

But it's weird right?

You remember how much she hated Liz.

It's weird that Mason is hanging out with her.

Cade: Yeah it is.

But don't worry about this stuff babe.

Focus on good stuff.

Focus on us.

And college acceptance letters. Hoping we're near each other next year.

Bailey: You're right.

I should go to bed.

See you in the morning!

Cade: Shit.

I forgot to tell u.

I can't drive u tomorw.

I have to go in early for a makeup test.

Bailey: I'll be waiting at your locker, then. ☺

Night.

Cade: Good night.

CAUGHT UP

I get to school early, and my hat's not even off before I hear the sound of Mason's bee-buzz laugh echoing through the halls from the art room. I glide my fingers across the line of lockers that lead to his class—filled with people's lives and books and secrets—like they're going to navigate a path straight to him.

His laugh reminds me so much of Vanessa, and how she'd do anything to hear it. Like the time she danced a duck walk down the hall last year when he heard his mom's flight got delayed and she wouldn't be back for the end-of-the-year art showcase.

My feet slide across the floor outside the art room when I hear another just as recognizable voice with him.

I lean against the locker closest to the door, closing my eyes, listening as Liz says, "You've got to tell her at some point."

My stomach lurches, and I just know I'm the "she" in this sentence. The same way I knew something was wrong the night Vanessa died. I feel it as clear as the sensation of falling I have every time I wake up from one of those nightmares I keep having.

I don't hear exactly what he says but Liz replies, "You shouldn't have to keep this a secret."

"She's not ready." He's not wrong. I'm not ready for any of this. I'm not ready for Vanessa to be gone, or for him to move on. Especially with Liz.

The ringing in my ears echoes so hard I cover them, thinking back to all the times I came right to this room after school to find Vanessa because I knew she liked to hang out here and sit on the table and pretend to be his muse.

I'm lost in the moment, remembering one particular day when we stayed for an hour, mesmerized as we watched Mason on the pottery wheel, throwing coffee mug after coffee mug. How she tried her hand at it, and even with Mason's help it ended up in a blob he reworked into something beautiful.

I slip out of the daze only when I hear their footsteps approach.

Shit. My heartbeat thunders like the bass at a metal concert and I'm front row. I don't have time to move, much less think of something to do where it wouldn't look like I was just standing here listening in on their conversation. So I don't even try.

I'll always, always remember the way they appear in the hall— mid-conversation, her walking out backward, while he follows with his hands stuffed into his hoodie pockets.

She catches me first. Her lips part in a confused stare, attention returning to Mason in an "oh shit" expression. I can feel the way his eyes move to me—no confusion—it's guilt written in his eyes.

Or worse, maybe pity.

"I'm gonna go," Liz says, brushing a hand over his shoulder before stepping away. Very clearly giving him some now's-your-chance-to-tell-her-about-us eyes.

"No." I almost spit out the words. "I'll go. See you later."

And I go.

I dart off quickly, and Mason doesn't try to stop me. I'm practically running down the hall until I'm at Cade's locker. Closing my eyes, I take a moment to catch my breath and wait for things to slow down. For my heart to find a regular beat again. Maybe the answer isn't in finding out where she was going or why Mason and Liz are all of a sudden a thing. Maybe the answer is staying in rewind, because things were so much easier in the past.

Easier with Cade to get lost in.

Easier with V to share those old memories with.

Easier to forget the accident ever happened and I ever had something I needed to move on from.

Cade: Night babe.

Bailey: it's early!

Cade: Early practice.

Big game soon.

u coming?

Bailey: Yes!

Wouldn't miss it.

Cade: Cool.

Night babe.

Bailey: Night ☺

Esther: Soooooo

Random.

But I got that car!

Lolol

Bailey: That's awesome!

Esther: I posted a pic if you want to go see!

My parents knew I was saving up.

And my birthday is next month.

So they surprised me by matching my down payment as an early gift.

It's used but I'm SO excited!

Bailey: You should be!

It's so cool!

I just looked.

Congrats!

Esther: Anyway

Lolol

Do you want a ride to school Monday?

I'm dying to show it off.

Bailey: Absolutely!

7:10?

Esther: See you then!

Bailey: remember last year when we drove out to Seward on our own?

V: yes!

mermaids for life!

Bailey: I thought it was going to be weird going to the festival without my moms.

V: but it wasn't!

Bailey: Not even a little!

Cade and Mason were supposed to come too.

But you said you wanted it to be just the two of us.

V: that's right!

you were so pissed!

Bailey: Hey my moms and I had JUST gotten home from looking at schools.

I hadn't hung out with Cade in like a month.

Forgive me for wanting more than five minutes with him before we went to Seward.

Anyway, you stole some beers from your dad's stash and we took them out to the dock and drank and made new wishes.

V: like every year.

what did we wish for again?

Bailey: Well, I was feeling pretty angry that my mom had her "come to Jesus" chat with me while we were gone when she told me I screwed around junior year to hang out with Cade and that I was going to need a miracle to get into college.

V: heh.

i do remember this.

Bailey: Yep.

And the whole reason she wanted to take me on that trip was to show me what I'd have to work for because she knew if she didn't I wouldn't get my grades up.

And I bitched a whole lot about how hard it is to be Jacky Pierce's daughter.

V: yes. and if i remember correctly, how she'd had your schools picked out before you were even born, and you could not help that your grades didn't reflect your intelligence.

Bailey: Wow.

No wonder you didn't tell me about your breakup with Mason.

I bitched a whole lot on that trip, didn't I?

V: yes.

Bailey: Anyway.

Back to the wishes.

I held your hand and took a huge breath before I screamed.

Wishing on every inch of the unexplored ocean that Jacky-Mom could just be proud of me for once.

V: what did I wish for?

Bailey: You know . . .

You got so quiet.

237

I could hear the waves lapping against the wooden pier. And you took a deep breath.

Vanessa, I haven't even thought of this moment until now, but I was actually scared, because you looked out into the water, and you had tears in your eyes. You were squeezing my hand so tight I thought you were about to hit me with bad news.

V: what did you think i was going to say?

Bailey: I jumped to every conclusion.

At first I thought you were going to tell me your parents got divorced.

Then I panicked. Thinking you got your wish, and you were moving to Florida.

I even considered that while I was gone those two weeks you found out you had cancer and were dying.

That would have been the book girl way to go.

V: gotta love sick lit.

Bailey: But when you finally made your wish, you didn't do our thing.

V: what do you mean?

Bailey: You didn't scream your wish. You closed your eyes tight, and the tears in them spilled over your cheeks and . . . wow this is so sad.

V: what?

Bailey: you

V: oh em eff double gee lady! the suspense!!!!

Bailey: You stole my wish.

You wished we could be friends until we died.

V: awwwwwww! see you're my favorite human! i'm so glad
we have each other, you asshole. ☺

Bailey: Me too, you asshole. ☺

V: looks like we both get to keep our wishes.

THE SEWARD BUTTON

The green octopus button, on the right hem of her jacket, was found on the ground outside a diner we stopped at the day after we made those wishes. Our server was a slender girl with a short black pixie cut and a tattoo of a leaf on her forearm. Vanessa told her it was pretty as she took our order.

"Oh, thanks. I'm actually getting it covered next week. I got it with a friend," she said, looking at her arm and grimacing the way people do when they're remembering something sad. "And, uh, we're . . . not exactly friends anymore."

"My mom's really into gardening and stuff," Vanessa said, and I could tell she was about to say something she thought was profound because she leaned back in her chair, setting the menu down and looking up with all the intensity she could muster—that megawatt smile traveling into her eyes. "She always tells me that leaves are the best fertilizer. There's this whole thing about how leaves fall from the tree, and then they fertilize the ground, that ends up helping the tree grow. Maybe that's just a leaf you needed to shed so you could grow?"

The girl paused, still looking at the tattoo, but her eyes lit up. "Yeah, dude. I really like that. Maybe I'll keep it."

I'm holding her jacket right now, and can't stop thinking about how this isn't like shedding the leaves to move forward and grow. It's like my leaves have been plucked too soon, stolen and shoved into a plastic bag, and I'm stuck. Unable to grow because the fertilizer I should have had is missing. Gone. Empty.

Choking back a sob, I let my face fall into it, expecting it to smell like her—the combination of Mason's body spray and pages of old books—but it doesn't anymore. After months in my possession, it now smells like the candles Kat-Mom burns in my room when I'm at school. But also stale, like it needs to be washed.

Even her jacket has changed, and yet I'm still here. Stuck in every memory of every pin and no one to talk to about it.

My eyes sting, burning with tears that I fight at first but eventually allow. And it feels good, almost like my heart is having its very own exothermic release. I give in, letting myself feel every agonizing knock at the door to my memory.

Knocking.

There's knocking, and it takes me a moment to realize it's happening again. I look toward the window, covered with blinds, but the knock behind them grows louder. By the time I toss Vanessa's jacket aside and wipe my face with my sleeve, I've reached the opening. I pull the cord on the blinds, and they rise to reveal Mason standing there in the dark.

His eyes are wide. With tears in the corners, or maybe snow? I can't tell. But his chest rises and falls, his palm pressed to the window, a green duffel bag slung over his shoulder. It doesn't matter that I can't hear him. I know what he's mouthing.

"I don't want to be alone."

A BOB ROSS GOOD-NIGHT

I let Mason in.

I don't have to ask him what's wrong, and he doesn't ask me why my face is puffy and red. We sit on my bed, and he holds her jacket, turning it over in his hands until he gets to the spot on the sleeve where the forget-me-not pin used to live but doesn't anymore.

Like even Mason can't pretend we're both not thinking about where she could have been that night.

He doesn't ask if he can stay, but I pull out the trundle bed that's only been used by Vanessa. He sets his laptop on my nightstand while I unearth the extra bedding from the back of my closet—bedding I was sure I'd never use again. I pretend I don't see him close out the Facebook page with Vanessa's face on it and pull up Netflix.

He settles in, lying on his stomach and pressing play on a recently added episode of Bob Ross. I slip onto my bed, clutching a pillow while we watch in absolute silence. I'm burning with questions—the easy ones like why is he here tonight, and the hard ones like what is going on with Liz.

"I tried to call her today. I wanted to hear her voice on the voice-mail." He turns to me, his cheekbones outlined by the screen. "They turned off her phone, Bailey. Like they've moved on or something."

"Aren't they supposed to?" I ask. The silence between us so heavy it feels like fog. You can see through it, but it's hard. "Isn't that what we're all supposed to be doing?"

"I'm not moving on." The pain in his voice doesn't betray him. It's raw.

"But Liz," I say before I can even think about holding back. When his eyes dart to me, confusion written in his stare, I sigh. "Mason, I heard what she said. About needing to tell me."

"Okay, okay, listen." Mason looks like a marionette with a string pulling him to a seated position on the mattress. "I know how that probably sounded."

"How I'm not ready to know about you two?"

"It's not like that, Bailey." His shoulders slump, like the very string that brought him up has now gone limp.

"What's it like, then?" I can feel the sting of tears behind my eyes. "It's okay if it is like that. If you like her, I get it. I mean, it sucks that it's *her*, but I get it."

"Trust me. She's a friend. As soon as they move in, she's having a big housewarming party and you can come with me. You'll see. Friends."

My mom does this thing when she therapizes me. Where she'll purposefully stay silent when I'm waiting for her response. Knowing well that I'm a human and will do almost anything to fill awkward silence.

I don't even realize I've done the same thing to Mason when he starts talking again.

"We weren't good." He struggles with that last word. "There at the end. She'd been acting so strange for months. And I—"

"I know she broke up with you," I blurt out. He flinches at my words, looking toward the window.

"I didn't know she told you," he says, as if it's so exhausting he has to exhale the whole sentence. "Did she tell you what I did? What I said?"

"No."

"I'm not proud. I was desperate, though. Bailey, I didn't want to lose her." The tone in his voice goes frantic, his eyes widening as he realizes the weight of what he's saying. "I was so scared of being alone and having no one to go to that I said a lot of stuff I'm not proud of. I told her that—"

The day Cade broke up with me, the way I grasped at straws trying to convince him not to end it. I'd have said anything to make him understand how badly it hurt. To get a response. I wouldn't want anyone to know how hard I pressed, and now as Mason puts his hands on his face, I see what he's trying to say.

"You don't have to tell me what you said." I move to the edge of the bed, feet dangling over the trundle he's on.

"It doesn't matter." Mason speaks like there's no life left in his voice. "We got back together a couple days later. She said she didn't want you to know because you were stressed about schools and your moms. I think I begged too hard. Guilted her into staying. Like she was still in it, but we were never the same after that."

"That sounds like her."

"She never wanted to hurt people. Even if it meant . . ." Mason pauses, like he's thought it so many times it's part of him now, but never wanted to say it out loud. "Even if it meant staying with someone she didn't love anymore."

The heartbeat of the room dies.

I don't know what Mason's thinking as he turns Bob Ross back on, but I don't say another word. Eventually, after I hear him murmuring in his sleep, I close the laptop and tuck myself into my bed. With his eyes closed, he looks so peaceful. Like the last few months haven't been full of sighs and heartbreak.

Bailey: I've been thinking.

V: tell me more.

Bailey: You always did a good job of protecting me.

V: you protected me too!

that's what friends do.

like when you quit ski.

Bailey: It's this thing I always loved about you.

How fierce you are.

Like you always try to do the right thing. Even if it means things are harder for you.

V: you're gonna make a girl blush.

Bailey: That's why I can't stop thinking about that night.

When you left my house.

And where you went.

But mostly, I keep asking myself who you were protecting.

Was it me?

Mason?

Someone else?

V: i don't know.

bailey you have to stop asking.

i don't remember.

WEEK EIGHT

MOMS

We sit in the dining room sipping coffee like *Gilmore Girls* before school, Jacky-Mom locked into her iPad, looking up to show off a meme she found. "My friend's sister works at Stanford and said they are conducting interviews in the next few weeks. You haven't gotten an email or anything about that?"

I shake my head, looking up from my phone, where I'm messaging V.

"I think we're going to have an early spring." Kat-Mom stares out the window, hopeful as she waters the succulents and herbs she keeps behind the kitchen sink. She must see something I don't because my world is still fog and winter and ice. There's no escape, and I can't see farther than the space right in front of me. There's no Stanford here.

Kat-Mom says something about how we are glued to our screens, and she wants a tech-free night soon—something she demands every few months when she feels like we aren't connecting enough. I stare down at my phone, expecting the sinking feeling to take over my stomach the way it does when she talks about a break.

But it never comes.

Texting V is like sitting in the middle of a foggy meadow, only able to see my hands in front of me as I try to navigate my way out. I want to tell her everything. How Mason whimpers her name in his sleep. How his hair is grown out even longer than it was during quarantine, back when our bubbles were just each other and our boyfriends. How he was gone before I even woke this morning, and the only evidence he was ever there was a fully made bed and a green duffel stuffed in my closet.

But saying those things means admitting to V that she's dead.

Then the fog will have cleared, and the secrets will stay hidden forever.

FOUND

Esther picks me up for school as planned.

I gush about her car. A small sedan that she's already named Fox Mulder. Apparently, she's really into *The X-Files*, and by the time we get to school I've agreed to watch the first episode with her this weekend.

And for the most part, this all feels normal. Dropping our things off at our lockers, making Saturday plans. Hanging out with Esther is a little like putting on a pair of socks straight out of the package. The banter feels stiff, because it's brand-new, but cozy and warm nonetheless. We've bridged the gap from acquaintance to real friends.

On our way to class, we pass Liz and the rest of the Ski Squad cackling and carrying on about the "Countdown to SPRING BREAK" signs they've put on their lockers to announce to everyone in school that they're all meeting up in Aspen for a trip during break. Sophomore year, one day when she was particularly salty and the sign said Vail instead of Aspen, Vanessa ripped it down after school.

Liz attempts a smile in my direction, and I almost allow myself the polite grin that Esther flashes back, but keep walking.

The entire day is much more tolerable knowing that I'm not walking the halls alone. It feels like driving out beyond the inlet when the fog is low, but there's this one ray of sunshine peeking through the cloud. A hint of what beauty sits beneath.

All the feelings that keep me trapped in the fog are there, but seeing a tiny sliver of light makes today feel different. Hopeful.

We turn down the hall that leads to the science rooms, and I look over my shoulder toward the art room, an involuntary movement. Wondering if Mason is feeling the same splintering of normal today. Maybe there's something to Kat-Mom's insistence that I talk about my feelings.

"Looking for Mason?" Esther asks.

I shake my head, turning my attention back ahead of us. When I do, something catches my eye. It's so tiny and minuscule that it shouldn't even register, but it's like I'm reading one of those old Where's Waldo? books. Amid all the chaos of the halls, with people talking and running to and from their classes, I find Waldo and I wasn't even looking.

"What's going on?" Esther asks as I stop, blood rushing to my head, reaching for her arm to steady myself as she huddles in next to me like we're conspiring. "What is it?"

I have to squint my eyes and lean forward to make sure I'm seeing it right. A small blue enamel pin stuck onto a backpack. Blue petals, yellow center. Vanessa's pin.

After almost two months of wondering where it went, it's right here, bobbing up and down on someone's backpack, taunting me.

I can feel a burning sensation in my chest, my fingers tightening on the straps of my own backpack, like it'll help keep me from falling over.

"Bailey?" she asks, but I'm already gone.

I follow the backpack down the hall, and the guy wearing it is tallish and has a green baseball hat on. I push past people like a fish upstream, bouncing between hockey players who storm the commons, all dressed up in ties and dress shirts for the game tonight. Slipping through the crowd, I hear Cade say my name, then "babe," then something else, but I rush past, ignoring him.

I'm close enough to reach out and touch it. My heart beats a thousand times a minute and for a second, I swear I can hear Vanessa behind me telling me to stop. That I'm losing my mind. That it's nothing.

But I don't care.

Because it's right there. Her pin, just as real as it was when she wore it on her jacket.

I grasp a strap on his backpack and pull, and somewhere behind me, Esther says something, but it's too far away. Too slow, like the whole world is moving a frame at a time and everything she says is in that weird, deep slow-motion voice.

Motionless, I watch as the owner of the backpack comes flying backward. Turning frame by frame, he pulls his hat into his hand and I recognize the logo right away. Jordon Contracting. He lets it fall to his side before looking down at me. I stop breathing, waiting for my eyes to focus so I can see who it is. And after a million years, I do see him. Tight, curly hair. Light brown eyes. Warm sandy brows fixed in a confused stare.

Spencer Jordon.

He pulls away from me, straightening his shoulder strap. "What the hell, Bailey?"

"Where'd you get it?" I practically scream. Esther's caught up with me, breathless and panting by my side.

"What?" He looks at her, then behind her to Cade, who has caught up with us too.

"The pin on your backpack. The forget-me-not pin," I say. If I see anything in his face that resembles recognition, it's gone before it even fully forms. "It's not yours."

He pulls his backpack around until it's hanging off his chest. There are other pins there. Some band, a patch, and one from a national park—but next to them it's there—Vanessa's pin.

"This?" He yanks it free, holding it palm up, presenting it to me.

This piece of her I've been searching for. Now I'm searching Spencer's eyes. The dark center that splinters into honey—eyes that belong to the person who might be able to tell me where she was going that night.

"Bailey." Spencer says my name like an apology.

He looks behind me, lips parted, like he's waiting for words to fall out but doesn't know what to say. I turn; Cade is standing there, staring in disbelief. Next to him, Esther doesn't peel her eyes from the Tundra Cove High logo on the floor beneath her.

When I turn back to Spencer, he's slipping the pin into my hand. "I found it a few months ago on the ground and thought it looked cool. I'm so sorry. I had no idea it was hers."

Bailey: I found your pin.

V: what?

where?

Bailey: Spencer Jordon had it.

V: what?

Bailey: Apparently he's the kind guy who would find someone else's pin and put it on his backpack.

V: okay so he's quirky.

Bailey: You know what sucks?

V: a vacuum.

heh.

see what i did there?

Bailey: I thought for a second. Just a stupid brief second.

That I was finally going to know what happened.

As soon as I saw it I chased him down.

I chased him Vanessa.

I grabbed him and looked him in the eye because I was so sure that if I could find that stupid pin I'd have some answers.

And I got nothing.

And I'm so tired of feeling empty.

Trying to figure out this whole messed up puzzle, and being the only person who can't let it go.

258

Who can't move on.

V: whoa.

okay.

you're upset.

let's skip our next class. meet me for pop rocks?

Bailey: I wish.

V: i wish too.

GAME ON

After my last class I waited fifteen minutes before heading to my locker so I could avoid the rush after school. The shrine is long gone. A reminder that she's just a memory to most people, as transparent at the leftover tape that once held her picture.

I twist in the combination to my locker, swinging it open before I reach inside for my bag. Slipping the strap over my shoulder, I grab my beanie as a set of paint-splattered shoes comes scuffling toward me. There's no need to look up as I put my hat on. I know who they belong to.

"Hey." Mason's voice is hoarse and slathered in sympathy.

"You heard?" I stuff a book on the top shelf, reaching for another.

"The TCHS whisper network is strong." His smile is lopsided as he rests his head on my locker. "You okay?"

I'm so tired of that question.

"Mason," I say through a deep breath, trying to steady the thought that there will never be a time or place where I will feel okay. "I can't do this."

"Can't do what?" He's so close I can feel the whisper leave his lips. And I can't shake the image of him sleeping—whimpering her name like he was reliving the same scary nightmare I do. His smile is long gone, replaced with nothing but concern. "Talk to me, Bailey."

And I want to. I want to talk to Mason. I want to leave right now, sit on my bed and watch Bob Ross and tell him everything. He's the only other person who knows what's it like to live in the constant shadow of Vanessa's brightness. Who knows what it's like to be stuck in time with the memory of someone whose last words were a lie.

"Mason," I say, following his gaze over my shoulder, where Cade approaches.

I don't know why my stomach feels tied in knots when I see him. He's wearing his favorite dress shirt and a tie with molecules on it that I gave him at Christmas last year. I used to love game days because he looks so good.

"I've been looking all over for you," he says through a tired smile. Mason takes a step back while Cade slides up to my side, kissing my temple and resting his hand on my back. "What's up, bro?"

"Not much. Just leaving, actually. Good luck at the game tonight." Mason's eyes don't move away from us until he turns down the hall. I can hear a sort-of laugh bee-buzzing as he adds in a "bro" at the end.

THE END

Cade only communicates in heavy sighs and grunts until we climb into his truck. The auto-start has warmed it enough that the first thing I do is pull my beanie off. He tosses the key fob in the center console and rests his head against the chair, tilting it toward me with a frustrated stare.

"What's going on with you and Mason?"

I let a laugh slip before I realize he's serious. Swallowing the remainder of the laugh, I blink in response to the question. "What are you talking about?"

"Back there." He gestures toward the school. "What was that about? You guys looked like you were having a pretty serious conversation."

"Cade," I say before my lips clamp down in a thin line. "Mason's my friend. He was checking on me after . . ."

I have no idea how to finish my sentence.

He scoffs, rolling his head toward the windshield. "Okay, so what was *that* about? Going after Spencer? Over a pin?"

Anger bubbles hot in my chest, overheating my limbs.

"Cade." I say his name like it's the most important word I have. Like it'll make him understand the weight of what I need to say. For months, I've tiptoed around my grief like I'm walking across a lake after winter's first freeze. Now it's like I've broken the ice; I'm slipping under and screaming. "Something happened that night."

"Why can't you let it go?" He doesn't have the same "I'm sorry" eyes from the breakup, but they're just as tired, and they pierce me before the words unravel every thought I've been holding in.

Let it go. Like it's so easy to ignore the lie, pretend that whatever reason she had for dishonesty didn't directly affect me. How knowing would end the agony of wondering if there was anything I could have said or done to change the outcome of that night.

To know where that lie landed in our friendship.

If it would change us.

"Because she was my best friend," I finally say. "And someone knows where she was going that night."

"Yeah, okay." Cade reaches for my hand, eyes locked on me and filled with desperation. "I get it. I get that you're upset and you want answers. But you can't go around assaulting people—"

"—I did not assault Spencer."

"You ran the guy down, Bailey." Cade's thumb rubs against the top of my hand. "At some point you've got to move on, babe. Move forward."

"No." The word comes out before I have a chance to think. It feels like relief to finally say it. "She was my best friend. We were laughing and talking and joking like we always do, and then all of a sudden she wasn't. And I didn't ask her why. And I didn't tell her to stay even though something was bothering her. I didn't stop her, even though we'd been drinking, and I'll never stop wondering if it was me or the champagne or my text that—"

"Okay, okay." Cade's hands slip away from mine. He's rubbing both through his jet-black hair, mussing it as he stares out to the snow freckling his windshield with tiny flakes. "Bailey, what if you never know? Is this something that's going to live with you forever?"

My heart stops, because I can hear what he's saying with the question. *Is this who you are now?*

"I don't know. Maybe? Is that a bad thing? That I want to know?"

He shakes his head, "No. It's not bad, Bailey. It's . . ."

I can read the subtext here too. *It's just not what I want.*

I think about all the times we talked about our future, schools we could go to. Plans we were making. How it still doesn't make sense, only now I'm seeing why. It never had anything to do with schools or our future or how little I cared.

It's how I wasn't fitting into the mold he had in mind for what *his* future looked like.

"Why did we break up, Cade?" I ask.

He turns, thrown by the question. Hesitating before repeating the words he's already said. "Because I wasn't sure about schools. And I thought it would be easier if we weren't making those kinds of decisions with each other in mind."

"Come on," I said. "Just say it. It's okay. It's me, right? You didn't want to make decisions with me because I'm the thing you weren't sure about."

His chin tucks down to his chest.

We aren't in rewind anymore but fast forward. Barreling at warp speed through the last three months, four months. Everything I've been hiding from with Cade is staring me right in the face.

It starts in my chest—this sinking feeling—like losing a saved file or realizing you didn't back anything up after hours of working on a project and your laptop dies. It spreads, a virus through my arms and legs and fingers and toes. And those fingers that were wrung around my beanie are now limp in my lap as our tears echo between us.

The cord in my heart has been ripped out of the socket, and I can't stop living in the memory of a relationship that was broken any more than I can live in the memory of a person who isn't here.

When Cade finally looks at me, he's "I'm sorry" eyes all over again. His tone changes. It's not exhausted anymore, and it's desperate. He says he wants to forget this whole fight, he kisses my forehead, and he's doing and saying all the right things. Like he didn't pull back the scab that sat in the place of my heart where I kept this breakup. Slipped a knife over scar tissue that I've tried so hard to heal.

Cade has his mouth to mine, like he's trying to resuscitate my heart. But he's breathing life into lungs that won't work anymore. Vanessa's words ring in my ears like they're the pulse between me and Cade and everything else. *It's called a breakup because it's broken.*

"I can't." My hands find either side of his face. My forehead pressed against his, eyes closed, and his chin tilts toward mine. And I know what happens next. We kiss, and we kiss again, and I let myself slip back into comfortable love, and I forget all the reasons we shouldn't.

"I'm sorry," I say, hopping out of the car before I hit rewind again.

Bailey: Cade and I just broke up.

I mean.

Not that we ever officially got back together, but yeah.

V: ouch. omg bailey.

are you okay?

want me to come over?

we can have a repeat of last time.

get drunk.

eat candy.

want me to call mason?

he can get us beer i think.

Bailey: You have no idea how much I wish this was a reality.

That any of this was actually possible.

V: breakups are so hard.

Bailey: You know what's messed up?

I'm, like, numb I guess.

Like this whole time maybe I knew it wasn't going to last.

I wasn't walking around like Cade and I are End Game.

Breaking up this time is like seeing a grade from a test I knew I bombed.

But I'm not heartbroken the way I was the first time.

Still . . .

V: still?

Bailey: I don't know.

Frustrated?

Pissed I can't do this with you.

V: okay.

i'm coming over.

i'm not taking no for an answer.

get ready.

you. me. booksmart. pop rocks.

BREATHING

My fingers are numb by the time I walk through the door to my house. Cade followed me for a while in his truck, asking if he could please drive me home, but eventually he got the picture and drove off.

After that it was me and my friend winter—every snowflake dotting a path home like Hansel and Gretel following a path of bread crumbs to warmth.

Even my toes burn, tingling like they've fallen asleep up to my ankles, and when the warmth of my home hits, it feels worse. I shake off the chill, throwing my coat on the floor even though I know Kat-Mom will yell at me for it later.

I bend at the knees to grasp my toes so they'll stop the burning when Jacky-Mom walks in from the kitchen wearing a pair of jogging pants and an oversized shirt that says, "This is my work-from-home shirt." Judging by the look of her unkempt hair, she's been doing just that. Sitting in her office most of the day, snacking on gluten-free pretzels and enjoying the silence of winter.

"When will this stop?" I ask. "The hurting. I need to know when it stops."

It feels like watching an avalanche form. I've done nothing to stop the growth of snow backed up in my heart. Nothing to stop the snowfall from accumulating. Now I'm staring at the drift as it tumbles at Mach speed, and I'm in a direct path of its chaos.

And it happens. I clutch my knees, tears pouring out of me like snow passing down the mountain. Pulling my emotion trees from their roots, dislodging the ways I've ignored all these feelings for so long. I sob, giant body-shuddering sobs.

It doesn't matter that Jacky-Mom never answers, because I know the truth is clear.

It will never stop hurting.

She'll never be back.

We'll never laugh again.

Or eat Pop Rocks or scream our wishes out to sea.

She's gone.

Esther: Hey! I don't have to work tomorrow, and I was thinking . . .

I've never been to one of the hockey games. Do you want me to go with you? We can make signs!

It'll be fun!

Bailey: Yeah. That would be fun.

But Cade and I kind of broke up today.

Esther: OMG BAILEY!

ARE YOU OKAY?

What happened?

I'm so so so so so so so sorry.

Do you want me to come over?

Bailey: I promise I'm okay.

I'm eating ice cream.

And my moms just pulled out the board games.

Can I text later?

Esther: Absolutely.

Let me know if you want some company tonight.

Bailey: I'm probably going to hang out with my parents.

Thank you though.

I'll text tomorrow.

INCANDESCENT STARES

That night, after hours of board games with my moms and a long call with Esther where I gave her the gruesome details of the breakup right down to those final moments in the car, Mason came over.

I had the trundle bed pulled out before he even knocked, hair filled with snowflakes before he stepped into my room. Watching him shake off his coat like a wet Labrador, the knot in my stomach fades, and I realize I've been looking forward to this.

We could pick up our almost conversation at the lockers.

I could tell him all the things that led up to the moment with Spencer. Pull from the texts I stole from his phone. Tell him how tired I am, and how holding the glue of Vanessa's memory together with a bot is exhausting. Reveal every gruesome detail of my breakup with Cade.

But we don't do any of those things.

Instead, I set my laptop on the nightstand, Bob Ross queued and ready to go. This time we watch side by side between throw pillows and a stuffed sloth I've had since I was a kid.

And I keep waiting for the uncomfortable part. The conversation part. But he presses play and Bob goes on like he does in every episode. My nerves dissipate like the snowflakes falling beyond my window. We laugh when Bob says something related to trees being happy, or filled with squirrels, or crooked so he was going to send them to Washington.

Bob starts a new painting by coating the canvas in a base color, then adding details as he goes. A mountain range here, a stream filled with fish there. We watch as he outlines the first tree and moves to the second. "Gotta give him a friend. Everybody needs a friend."

"I'm glad we're friends, Bailey." Mason looks over at me, smiling through his eyes and hovering on a beat.

There's a moment here where his smile disappears, and I can feel a shift between us as instant as a sparked flame.

The color of a flame is indicative of a few things. Temperature, the type of fuel, and how complete the combustion is. His eyes move on me, an alkane blue flame, complete combustion that is perfect and pure and studied. We know exactly what this is.

But as his eyes move down to my mouth, that same blue flame transforms to yellow. It's breathless and starved of air, incomplete combustion. There's tension here, and his stare—incandescent. Incomplete energy filled with so many emotions it's hard to describe it any other way.

It's the kind of moment you wish you could snapshot. Hold on to. Take away with you because you know in ten years, you'll only remember it in fragments. And I'm champagne right now. Bubbles rising through my stomach and dancing their way all over every inch of my skin.

Bob's still jabbering in the background, but we're silent, and I swear I can feel the space between us getting smaller, like we're going to get closer and closer until we're not just sharing sad breaths but happy ones too.

I can hear a question in his eyes like it's being screamed. *Can I kiss you?*

My first thought, the one that comes right to the surface, is that I want this. I want to kiss Mason. I want to forget about this whole hell day. I want to kiss the only person I've been able to adequately grieve with because maybe if we kiss it'll fill whatever void I've been walking with.

My second thought, the one that comes right on the heels of the first—like that void is being smashed with brick—is that this would change everything.

We'd always be an incomplete combustion.

The weight of this shift hits me. How this feeling, this moment right here, would be perfect if it weren't my best friend's boyfriend. It's not incandescence anymore but all guilt, and the startling realization that maybe I wasn't the best friend I thought I was.

"Me too. I need a good friend," I say, emphasis on the word *friend*. Flattening all the bubbles between us, throwing water into the flame of the moment I never want to forget as long as I live.

GOING HOME

I spend breakfast on Saturday thinking about what a terrible friend I am because Vanessa's boyfriend has slept over three times this week. So when Jacky-Mom asks me if I want to take a drive, I jump at a distraction.

She's mostly quiet as we pull out of our driveway and leave the neighborhood.

It's not like neighborhoods in a subdivision. Yeah, our streets are paved and homes are spaced far enough apart that you can't see one house from the next. But there are more trees than people, and the paths between them are worn by foot instead of machine.

I can feel her pulse in that weird way you know someone wants to say something, but they don't know how to say it. Her lack of words lingers between us like snow between air and earth.

I rub my hands together, holding them to the vents.

"I need to apologize." She stares straight ahead, but I can tell she's looking at me out of her peripheral vision.

"For what?" I ask.

"I don't think I've done the best job helping you through all of this." I can tell it's hard for her to say it, because she keeps pushing blond tendrils of hair back behind her ears. "People like us have a harder time letting go of things."

"Mom. I promise we don't need to do this," I urge her. More than likely it isn't even a conversation she wants to have, but something Kat-Mom told her we needed to do.

She doesn't take the out.

"When your dad got sick, everything happened really fast. We got the prognosis, and a few weeks later he was gone. Those weeks were hell because I felt like all I could do was wait—either for him to die or for you to be born." She turns up the hill. Fog has settled between the trees and the ground and the farther we get, the thicker it seems.

"I, um, got really depressed after you were born." Mom didn't even cry when her nana died, but as she changes gears, I see little droplets of tears forming in her eyes.

I rest my hand on her arm, and she doesn't shake it off.

"To everyone else I seemed fine." Her voice is so timid and small it sounds like it doesn't belong to her. "I was running a company day in and day out, and doing everything I could to be a good mom because I felt like if I failed at either I was failing him. But every night after I put you to bed, I cried myself to sleep."

She turns the steering wheel, swallowing hard before going on. "Grandma and PopPop wanted you to stay over. It was the first night you weren't with me, and I realized while I was sitting there that I was so lonely. So sad. And I'm at the table just crying my eyes out when there's a knock at the door."

We hit another curve, and my stomach drops as the sign for Raven Pass comes into view. Just behind it, a yellow caution sign with little squiggles to let drivers know there are a lot of turns. My shoulders tighten, searching her face for some sign she made a mistake. "Wait. Where are we going?"

"That's when Kat stopped by to bring me something of his she'd found when she was moving. They'd been friends for so long, and she was missing him too. I don't even remember what it was. But after, we cried. A lot. Then your mom, that beautiful soul, loaded me up in the car and we drove out to his grave so I could say goodbye. And it helped. A lot. Saying goodbye, being around someone who loved him so much."

Her SUV snakes toward the edge of the road, parking feet away from a white cross stuck in the ground. It's not huge and ugly like the shrine on Vanessa's locker at school, but her initials and the date she died are etched in Mrs. Carson's beautiful Disney-like scrawl, a tiny forget-me-not painted next to it.

A memorial. A reminder. An ellipsis worthy of only the most bookish of girls.

"Mom—" I choke on my words, and my heart quickens. She wraps her arms around me and holds me as I sob into her shoulder. And for the first time ever, I feel like she gets me before I need to say anything.

FEAR OF FALLING

The stillness of the mountain startles my core. My stomach is tight and my arms straight, taut lines at my side. I try not to think about her last moments or what it must have felt like to fall over the edge. If she was scared. If she even had time to cry.

The mountains are gray and quiet behind us, and as far as I can see, treetops peek through the fog. I kneel next to the cross and trace the letters of her name there. Tapping a thumb over the forget-me-not.

Here lies the book girl who slipped away from our lives in the loudest way.

"Goodbye." My throat squeezes around the word like a hug. "Goodbye, Book Girl and senior year and the perfect prom."

Behind me, I can hear my mom sniffling up tears, trying to stay strong because she thinks it's what I need.

"Goodbye, wishes on boardwalks. Goodbye, drives to school. Goodbye, lunches on the stairs. Goodbye, sleepovers and telling each other everything. Almost everything. Goodbye, Pop Rocks. Good—" I wrap my arms around my stomach, pushing down the puffy coat

I'm wearing. "Goodbye, Vanessa."

In this moment, it doesn't matter if she was messy or flawed. Any secrets kept between us evaporated like mist in the sky. A period to dot a goodbye instead of this open-ended ellipsis left in my phone.

I stand, the knees of my pants soaked through with snow, and follow my boot prints back to the car with my mom. I'm already thinking of what it would feel like to text Esther and tell her we should hit that game anyway. How I could meet Cade outside the rink after, and what it might sound like to say I was ready to leave the mess as-is and forget the big fight and—more importantly—make our own incandescent moments after.

Because this doesn't have to be part of me anymore.

But then, as I pull the door open, I hear the crunch of snow on tires. A bright red van crawls down the mountain pass, heading into town. As it gets closer, I make out the logo on the side because I saw it yesterday on Spencer's ball cap. Jordon Contracting, responsible for every single "I'm sorry" remodel done at Vanessa's house.

And just like that, it clicks.

Bailey: I, my friend, have had an epiphany.

V: this always ends well.

Bailey: I can't believe I didn't see it before.

You were going to see Spencer that night.

V: again with spencer?

Bailey: Just follow me.

V: following.

Bailey: There are only five homes at the pass.

I researched all five, trying to figure out a reason you'd have driven up there. You didn't have connections to any of them except Liz.

V: ew.

Bailey: Exactly.

Which I kept thinking there's no way you'd go to her house, right?

V: right. we hate her.

Bailey: she's the worst.

V: okay so i'm failing to see how any of this is resulting in an epiphany.

Bailey: Liz's house was older. I know because I looked at pictures online and it's hideous. That's why they haven't moved in yet. Something I didn't even know until Mason mentioned it the other day.

V: aw my mason ♥

Bailey: Which means they had to have it completely remodeled.

V: okay . . .

Bailey: Then there was the pin thing.

He had your pin. Your favorite pin.

V: because he found it.

Bailey: A lie.

It absolutely had to be a lie.

Because today I saw Spencer Jordon driving down the pass, and THAT is the moment it clicked. His dad must be the one doing the remodel, which means he's been working on that house for months.

And you know him because of school, because he worked on your house too, right?

V: bailey.

tundra cove has a population of like 5 thousand people.

Bailey: 5,356.

Wait. No. 5,355.

V: either way, irrelevant.

we all kind of know each other is my point.

Bailey: But YOU were driving up the pass when you were supposed to meet Mason at your house.

Then you said you were held up with me. A lie.

Who held you up?

Was it Spencer?

V: no.

you're being ridiculous.

Bailey: No.

YOU are being ridiculous.

It makes sense.

Were you into Spencer?

Is that why you broke up with Mason?

Why would you be going up the hill that night otherwise?

V: this doesn't make sense.

after everything my dad put my mom through

i'd never cheat.

you know how i feel about cheating.

ANOTHER NIGHT, ANOTHER HAUNTING

Spencer is the only one standing between me and Vanessa's flaming car.

His eyes aren't the same pale brown they are in real life but so dark they're almost black, and the few freckles he has have somehow tripled. The forget-me-not pin is attached to the collar of his shirt, and he's got her copy of *Forget Me Always* clutched to his chest like it's an extension of him meant to be there.

Same hand clutching a forget-me-not flower, the other gripping her jean jacket.

He holds it like it knows his soul.

I'm watching him, but he's not looking back. He's somewhere else, gaze over my shoulder when I see tears start to form and fall down his face in little lines that look like winter rain. Cold. Heavy. Hidden behind something else.

I reach out for him, though I don't know why, but here in my dreams I feel so bad for him.

"Why do you have her book?" I ask, but he doesn't look at me.

I reach for him again, struggling against the weight of his body, and shake him. Hard. Trying to force something out of him the way an interrogator tries to get information from a criminal. It doesn't matter how hard I shake, or how I scream until my lungs are so empty I think I might pass out.

It's only then that he finally looks at me.

And as if I've fallen into the black pits in his eyes, everything goes dark.

Mr. Carson: Are you home right now?
I have something I'd like to drop off.
Bailey: I am.

PRETTY LIES

Mr. Carson sits in my driveway for ten minutes before he gets to the door. I know because I've been watching from the window since he texted. The snow that melted into a small pool at the base of the steps yesterday has now refrozen into a thick layer of ice.

He gets out of the car, one of those canvas shopping bags hanging from his fist, and by the time I meet him at the door he's brought it up to his chest, where he hugs it like there really is a piece of Vanessa hiding in the bag.

My heartbeat quickens as he pulls back the canvas bag, revealing a thin metal casing covered with as many stickers as she had pins. Her laptop. The mother lode of information. As much Vanessa bot food as there could be.

Here.

In his hands.

"Emily had it in our closet." Mr. Carson sighs, his lips twisting away the tears in his eyes. "She wasn't ready to let go of it yet." He has this soft smile, like it's silly, but his fingers curl around it with white knuckles before extending it to me. "You girls were so close, and I think she'd want you to have it."

"Are you sure?" I ask, and he responds by pushing it into my arms.

"Yeah. It's what she would have wanted," he says, turning his back and walking down the stairs.

"Mr. Carson—" I sputter his name and he stops to look over a slumped shoulder.

There's so much I want to say to him. I want to say I'm sorry. That if I could go back to that night, I'd tell her she couldn't go. But first, I'd go back so I could live every memory we had, because I loved all of her. Even the messy parts. Even the parts of her she didn't want me to see.

But I don't say any of those things. Just "Thank you."

"I know we had problems. I know I hurt her. I know I pushed her." His head bobs a few times, eyes forced shut like it'll brace him for what he says next. "I just hope she knew I loved her too. More than anything. I loved her."

"She knew," I say, because I'm not sure it's true, but I think it's the right thing to say.

Mr. Carson gets in his car without looking at me again. I watch from the porch as he pulls out of the driveway onto the main road. And I wait until it's all the way out of sight, and the sound of his snow tires on the wet ground has reverberated into the still of winter.

IN MY HANDS

After he's gone, I race to my room, slamming the door behind me.

I set Vanessa's laptop onto my desk and stare down at the jacket sitting on it. It feels like a literal piece of her—flesh and bone—left behind bloody and breathing. Jamming the charger cord into the side, I evaluate the stickers on the case. I get why Mrs. Carson would want to keep this hidden away in a closet, because there's part of me that wants to leave it like this.

Untouched.

All those pieces of her. Social media accounts. DMs. Texts. The Notes app where she kept all the rough drafts of her posts and texts she knew would be hard to send, as if keeping them and letting them age would make the blows easier. The homework assignments. The photos of books and mountains and friends. The pieces of Mason that also live here.

But the bigger part of me—the part that wins—is the part that knows whatever secret she hid behind the firewalls of this laptop will heal us. Once I have it, and I know for sure, we can all start to move on.

Resting my fingers on the keys, I can almost sense her energy. Knowing the last time they were touched was by *her* makes me feel a little better. A little closer. A little lighter.

The screen awakens, requesting her password. I click on it, typing in the same code she's had since a week after Mason asked her to be his girlfriend.

ilovemason

Hand to the stars, my whole galaxy falls from the sky when I see the error message on the screen. I try again. And again. I try other passwords too. The name of her first pet, a cockatiel named Tom Cruise, *Forget Me Always*, and just about anything else I can think of.

I click on the "hint" button, only it taunts me with a "who do you love, you asshole?!"

The exclamation point drives it home when I think about the way Mason said she didn't love him anymore. Like the password changed, but the hint stayed the same. As if Vanessa just copied and pasted someone new into her laptop the way she did in her life. Silently, hidden in plain sight.

I click back on the password prompt, the cursor blinking. Taunting. I know exactly what the new password is.

ilovespencer

I press "enter," closing my eyes for a moment and willing it to bring her screen to life with all those pieces of her I wanted to see. But it doesn't. Not this time.

WEEK NINE

NEWS

When I wake up, my eyes are swollen.

This time it's not from crying but from staying up too late staring at her laptop screen. I tried every password I could think of. *ilovebailey*, *iloveharrystyles*, *iloveaugustuswaters*, and every answer to her hint I can think of. I also found and downloaded an app online that predicts passwords and boasted a billion guesses per second.

I'd nodded off in front of the screen twice waiting for it to work, and finally went to bed.

Which is why I cringe when I follow the smell of coffee downstairs and Kat-Mom excitedly starts clapping. "There's our girl!"

Her smile is the same smile, accompanied by the same clap she gives when she's winning a board game. Jacky-Mom rolls her eyes from behind the screen she's glued to, but she's smiling too.

Kat-Mom hands me a cup, and I fall into the seat next to Jacky, clutching it like a lifeline. "We checked your grades this morning, and you're doing great. You're going to finish senior year out strong."

"That's not even the best part!" Jacky-Mom smacks my arm, and I groan in response. "I talked to my friend whose sister works at Stanford. She talked to Bianca Sawyerr, the woman in charge of applications!"

"Am I to assume this means good news?" I ask as Jacky-Mom slides a blueberry bagel in front of me.

"Well, she said they are just now reaching out to schedule interviews. I explained your situation, and she thought that you should have a decent shot despite the hardship you faced last year."

The word *hardship* slaps me in the face, but I fake a smile anyway. I fake everything that comes after. The celebratory coffee-mug-cheers with my moms. The excitement as I tell them I can't wait to kill that interview, because that's what Jacky-Mom wanted to hear, and go get ready for school. And the part I fake the hardest.

That I even care about anything except Vanessa's laptop and what secrets live on it.

HIM

Esther picks me up, and by the time we get to school we've discussed each other's weekends. She took my advice and binge-watched *Saved by the Bell*. Clearly, she's team Kevin to end up with Kelly Kapowski. I tell her about this morning with my moms—the interview, the grades—even the goodbye drive up the mountains.

Everything else I leave out. Mason, Cade, Spencer, the laptop.

When we get to AP Chem, the stations are rearranged with two tables pushed together to create groups of four. As people walk through the door, Mrs. Kamaka points to where she wants them to sit. She directs Esther and me to a seat near the middle, and I scan the rest of the room for Cade, but he isn't here yet.

The supplies set out in the center are a balloon, baking soda, and vinegar. Classic chemical-reaction assignment. When the bell finally rings, the entire class starts in on their experiments, and Esther doesn't miss a beat as she begins filling out the worksheet.

I almost reach for my phone to text Cade and ask if he's sick when I see the door at the front of the room open. Cade's cheeks are bright red as if he's been playing hockey or running. Spencer isn't far behind him.

Cade won't look at me, but Spencer does. Only for a second.

He's got hollow cheeks and dark circles beneath his eyes that flash a solitary glance in my direction before he looks away. And I know with every fiber-optic nerve that is flexed on him that Spencer's the one Vanessa was going to see that night.

He's the guy.

"Cade, Spencer," Mrs. K says, looking around the room before she lands on us. My heartbeat quickens, searching the room to find that we're the last table left. "You boys can sit with Esther and Bailey."

My whole body goes hot as they approach. Esther is already on the end of the table, and I'm closest to the center. That leaves one seat next to me, and another next to that one. It looks like they're running through the same logistics because Spencer's chin dimples and Cade leans into him, whispering.

A clear request that Spencer take the seat nearer to me. Spencer nods, but I can see him hesitate as he falls into place beside me while Cade takes the edge seat.

While Cade looks flushed, Spencer appears stunned. He chews on the corners of his thumbnail, and up close I can see beads of sweat forming on his neck. And it's like he knows, or at least suspects that I know. I'm seeing a whole new version of him.

He's not the guy who spent half a semester annoying my on-again, off-again boyfriend.

He's Vanessa's guy. The secret so important she lost her life to keep it.

WHAT WAS

While Mrs. K drones on about the assignment, I imagine the whole relationship between Vanessa and Spencer in fast forward.

He was working on one of those remodels. Maybe the kitchen update from last summer. Installing new countertops while Mrs. Carson looked on with that gloriously long hair, stringing a finger through the magnificent gray streak that makes her look a little like a superhero. Vanessa sat nearby, silently reading whatever book of the month showed up in her subscription box.

When Mrs. Carson left, he mentioned the bookcases from *that* remodel. They talked about their favorites. She felt seen. And oh, did Vanessa love to be seen. The next day he came back. She stayed in the kitchen, even if it was in shambles, and they talked about books while he worked.

A few days later, he brought her a copy of his favorite book. She shared hers too, telling him why she loved *Forget Me Always* so much, and after the project was finished, he kept coming back to trade stories with her.

They started texting. He's the one Vanessa texted her good-nights to, while Mason lay beside her every time his mom had an overnight flight.

But it didn't stop her from thinking about Spencer all the time, from texting him and talking about what it would be like if they could be together. And one night she watched their flame go from blue to yellow, only she did nothing to stop it. They kissed, and she felt so alive. Like all the wishing we did on the docks every summer finally paid off.

She was in love with Spencer.

But Mason still needed her, and even though she tried to break it off, she knew she couldn't. And Vanessa always, always took care of the people she loved. Even when it meant keeping Spencer a secret. Even when it meant keeping it from me and how that must have eaten her up inside.

We went to the beach.

She wished we could be friends until we died because she knew she was keeping this big thing from me. Vanessa hated it, and I hate the idea she might have felt that way too.

When we got home that weekend, she and Spencer held each other under starlit nights—kissing like the book girl she was. Beneath a blanket of the northern lights dancing green and blue like a light show meant just for them. Proof that their love was special.

And she pulled the pin from her jacket, slipping it into his hand so he'd have a piece of her when school started. Because, while she loved Spencer, she was still with Mason.

They were still the couple everyone looked at when they walked down the halls. People still noticed the way Mason smiled right before he reached for her hand, and that he kissed her nose when she was upset so he could hear her Boston terrier laugh.

The laugh Spencer thought was just for him. And when she was holding hands with Mason, she looked at Spencer, wishing it was his fingers laced with hers.

For a while it was enough that Spencer knew she'd go wherever he was. They could meet in secret, and she'd lie to anyone to steal a moment with him because all those moments were sacred. Incandescent. He was working on Liz's vacant house by then, and in the comfort of those big empty walls, they kept meeting.

Kept kissing.

Kept planning for what someday would look like once she and Spencer could be together. They imagined their future, wishing on starlight and secrets that they could have a forever so beautiful it would only be rivaled by the most epic of romances. It was enough for him to be her good-night text.

The night she died, he saw the post we all saw. Mason at the party. Thinking Vanessa had the night free, he asked her to meet him at Liz's. But then he saw her response. He didn't know Mason beat her to the invitation—he needed her that night.

How could Spencer know she'd risk anything to see him? Even if it meant driving up the pass and dying.

When she never came, he gave up. He even drove right past the ambulance and police parked and staring over the edge. And he will always, always have that lie—the heartache in his soul. Even as he sits here in class next to me, sweating and looking anywhere but into my eyes.

Spencer pulls his phone out. The one with all those good-night texts. Tapping in his code, he turns it away from me before typing something out. And I know right then, as Mrs. K is warning us we don't have much time to complete our experiment, that before I leave this room, I'll have done something just as unthinkable as keeping this secret.

Bailey: Make me a promise?

Esther: Anything.

Bailey: No matter what happens during the experiment.

DO NOT GET OUT OF YOUR SEAT.

Esther: What?

Bailey: Promise me.

I'll explain later.

Esther: Okay.

THE UNTHINKABLE

I measure out everything.

The vinegar from the bottle, the baking soda expertly placed inside the opening of the balloon. All four of us are wearing goggles, even though the boys are on their phones and hardly participating. Esther grabs her pencil, filling out the next portion of our worksheet.

Next up is the actual chemical reaction. I'll stretch that balloon on the lip of the bottle, the baking soda will then fall into the vinegar, thus creating a chemical reaction that will blow up the balloon. And if I can pull it off, create quite a mess.

"Guys, can you at least *watch* the experiment?" I roll my eyes. Both look up from their phones, and while Cade grunts in annoyance, he slips his phone into his pocket. But see, Spencer doesn't have pockets in the joggers he's wearing. He sets his phone right between him and Cade. Exactly where I want it.

I twist my neck from side to side, loosening my nerves as I grab the balloon. My hands tremble as I pull the opening around the lip of the bottle. I have to move quick and I've got one shot. I shake it out, watching as the vinegar begins to bubble.

I have to time this just right or it won't work.

The bubbles start fizzing their way up the side of the glass bottle like it's filled with Pop Rocks instead of everyday baking soda. I don't have time to check and see if either of them is paying attention. I tilt the edge of the balloon off the lip of the bottle, aiming it toward Spencer as the bubbles erupt from the top

"What the hell, Bailey!" Cade yells.

"What are you—?" Spencer steps back, hands in the air as the spray hisses out of the balloon and splatters all over him and the table.

"Shit!" I play it perfectly. The way my jaw opens, eyes wide in shock. The way my hand goes right up to my heart. "I'm so sorry!"

Spencer's nostrils flare, like he's exhaling his anger before his arms drop down to his sides and he stares at the mess all over his shirt. The desk. His phone.

"Get some paper towels!" I yell at Cade, and out of the corner of my eye I see Esther wiping the worksheet off with her sleeve as I reach for Spencer's arm. "I can't believe I did that, Spencer. I'm so sorry."

He waves it off, even though I can tell he's annoyed as he stomps toward the front of the room to ask for a hall pass. With both guys distracted, I grab Spencer's phone off the desk and shove it into my bag. By the time Cade gets back with a giant wad of paper towels, I'm zipping my bag and avoiding Esther's stare.

Because the way she looks at me—like I've just kicked a puppy in the face—makes my insides turn to jelly. Wobbling and unsteady as we all work to pick up this very intentional mess. Spencer isn't back by the time class is over, but Cade packs up his stuff anyway and sets it up front for Mrs. K to get to him.

I smile as I walk out of the room, knowing that this may be the real mother lode.

I don't wait for Esther. We don't participate in our leisurely stroll to our lockers so we can talk and make plans for lunch. Instead, I race to my locker until I'm breathlessly spinning the dial, popping it open it to grab my laptop.

I hear my phone chime with a text. Then another.

No doubt, it's Esther asking what the hell was I doing, but in a much nicer way.

I slip through the crowd, even passing Spencer wearing a TCHS gym T-shirt. I don't stop until I'm at the very back table of the library. Surrounded by books, it feels like Vanessa herself has given the blessing to do what I need to do.

I open my computer first, but while it's firing up, I tap in the four-digit code I watched Spencer use in class. My heart pulsates, thrumming on autopilot as I slip right into his messages app.

I don't think about girl code, and I don't care what lines I'm crossing.

The first name I see is Cade's. Even though this isn't what I'm after, I scan the little preview of their conversation and see "she doesn't know bro. it's not ur fault."

It's like I've gotten to the top of the roller coaster and I'm staring down into the drop and there's nowhere I can go but to click on the conversation and read the last few texts.

Spencer: I can't do this anymore.

She knows, doesn't she?

I'm going to tell her. I have to come clean. This is killing me.

Every time I look at her it feels like she's judging me.

Like she's blaming me.

God I feel so guilty.

Cade: calm down.

she doesn't know bro.

It's not ur fault.

Then an ellipsis; Cade is typing.

Cade: I left ur shit with mrs. K. don't worry abt Bailey. I'll talk to her.

Just stay cool ok

I think back to all the times Cade told me to drop it. To leave it. How he all but asked if I would ever give up on this.

My stomach turns over on itself as I exit out, tapping "Vanessa" into the search bar.

Her name appears, the preview message ripping my lungs right out of my chest.

Spencer: I'm sorry.

I open the thread with her. She's there as Vanessa "Book Girl" Carson. And beside her name there's an emoji with a stack of books because apparently Spencer is the kind of guy to take that amount of time to create a contact in his phone. Or maybe it's just for people he really cares about.

My throat struggles against the need to breathe.

He's texted her every day, too, only he doesn't have a bot to respond in her likeness. But his message is simple. *I'm sorry.* An apology every single day, time-stamped late, his good-night next.

Identical messages. I want to scroll through their history to see just how many "I'm sorry" texts he sent, but I can't bring myself to do it. Yes, I'm a thief, but one with at least enough resolve to hold back on reading all those personal moments. I plug Spencer's phone into my computer and start the upload to the bot.

By the time my next class is over, I'll have an updated version of the app, fully able to text back and forth so I can get the truth from V herself.

Esther: Where are you?

What was that about?

Why did you take his phone?

Bailey: I promise I will tell you later.

Esther: Today?

Bailey: Yes. Later today.

I'll explain everything.

Meet me at my locker after school.

Esther: K.

Bailey: Were you cheating on Mason?

V: bailey.

don't do this.

Bailey: You were, weren't you?

V: yes.

Bailey: After everything we've been through, you couldn't tell me?

V: you don't understand.

Bailey: And Spencer?

V: it wasn't supposed to happen the way it did, okay?

i can't make excuses.

i didn't want anyone to get hurt.

Bailey: Well someone got hurt.

A lot of people got hurt.

I'm so fucking mad.

We all got hurt.

You got hurt.

V: i don't want to do this over text.

can we talk in person?

NUMB

I thought it would bring relief, but instead I feel numb. Like my heart has been anesthetized and I'm incapable of feeling anymore. My hands could belong to someone else, void of any sensation as I go through the effort of powering down Spencer's phone. My phone. My laptop.

Until everything is as powerless as I feel in this moment.

I walk through the rest of the day a zombie. Trudging to my locker after school as if my boots are filled with stones. I open it, dumping my things in the bottom with little care because I have nothing left to feel.

The halls are filled with people scurrying like ants to get out of the building.

The Vanessa I remember doesn't exist anymore. Her locker is shrine-free, and those messages for the girl she wanted people to see are probably sitting in a landfill. She's not in my phone either, because I've ruined that by replacing her with V, who might be a bot but is still probably closer to the real version of Vanessa I thought I knew.

I wish I could go back to the beginning of the year when we were decorating our lockers and talking about what senior year would bring. How she designed her "locker look" the way she cultivated her Bookstagram posts—with the same shiny, flawless veneer she used in real life.

I twist her combination into her lock, pulling up on the silver handle. I want that version back—the pieces of her that would have recommended a bag of Blue Raspberry Pop Rocks as if they were doctor's orders instead of a fun anecdote she made up to put a smile on my face.

But it doesn't open. Even though I try again. And again, slamming my fist against the metal door like it'll free up a jam, pain radiating through my arm reminding me that I am not, in fact, as numb as I'd like to be.

At some point, Mr. and Mrs. Carson must have come to get her things. Maybe when they got rid of her phone. The school admin must have reset the combination to prepare for whatever lucky person gets to use it next year.

They really are gone, all those places Vanessa lived.

I slip back in with the ants, a bell ringing through the halls. I turn to see Mason up ahead. He's with his paint-splattered friends, and they swarm him on their way toward the art room.

His eyes fix on me, a stare stolen across the halls and over people. A stare silent to all the other ants, but that erupts like a sonic boom for me. Pulsating, bringing life back to my limbs. The same kind of stares Vanessa probably snuck with Spencer, looking through the commons while holding hands with Mason.

It's not "I'm sorry" filtered. It's "this hurts" filtered.

As simple and sad as him sneaking into my room in the middle of the night with snow-covered hair and a duffel bag over his shoulder. A look that says so much in nothing at all. That makes me feel like the motherboard to my heart has been fried and sold for parts.

CONFESSIONAL

Esther doesn't ask questions the way Vanessa did.

Best friend questions. The kind that go a little too far and don't let up when you're being cagey. The kind of questions I should have asked Vanessa the night she left my house.

When Esther meets me at my locker, she doesn't demand an explanation right away. We get in her car, and we're all the way back to my house, sitting in my bed with homemade granola bars that Kat-Mom left out, music playing over my Bluetooth speaker.

She doesn't hide her curiosity through a joke or press when the answer isn't good enough. Esther waits with painful curiosity, as if she wants to know so bad she'll burst and she's doing everything she can to keep it inside.

"We're friends, right?" I ask.

"Yeah." Esther's lips move over the word tentatively, almost like she already knows what I'll say.

"Remember that app I mentioned in STEM?" I stare out the window, the snowy landscape replaced with today's slush that will be ice in a few hours. I hesitate, mulling over memories where Vanessa might have sat like this, a breath away from revealing the truth.

"Yeah. The digital scrapbook thing?" she asks.

I pull Vanessa's jacket from the back of my chair and stare down at all the pins. Every story that made her who she was. I used to think it meant she wore her heart on her sleeve, but now leaves me wondering if it was her way of keeping people out.

A costume, a space to distract from everything inside.

"When Vanessa died, I used the app to talk to her. And I may have employed some less-than-stellar methods to get data for the app." I pull the forget-me-not pin off, turning it between my fingers as I look over to Esther. She swallows, hands in her lap as if she's bracing for impact. "I want to tell you what happened, but you have to know—"

"Hey." Esther cuts me off, sliding to the edge of my bed until we're face-to-face. "We're friends. Mistakes or not. You're my friend."

She doesn't smile or joke it out of me. Esther listens, nodding as I start from the beginning. Copying the app off my mom's laptop without her blessing, right up to today when she watched me steal Spencer's phone.

I tell her what I talked to V about and how sometimes having her in my pocket made me feel less lonely. And then how Mason sleeps here sometimes. I say right away that it isn't like that, but then say since I'm supposed to be honest, maybe it is a little like that.

I describe the incandescent moment and how I can't understand why she didn't just break up with him and stay broken up. That even V can't tell me why.

Esther never says a bad word about Vanessa, or V, or casts even so much as a judgmental stare. She just listens, handing me tissues while I cry, adding details as I go. Then, once I've exhausted every piece of the story, Esther makes me promise to give Spencer's phone back, her lips pinched in a motherly smile.

But she's there with no expectation. No filter on our friendship that prevents me from telling her the truth. And it feels so good to say it out loud, so much lighter, that I scoop her into a hug and thank her for understanding. Because everyone needs a friend like Esther.

And my greatest regret in life will always be that I wasn't that for Vanessa.

STERILE

In class, Mrs. K asked if anyone saw Spencer's phone yesterday after the experiment. Even though Esther was giving me mom eyes, and I could feel the phone in my jacket pocket, I stayed quiet. It's not until STEM Club is over, and with more than a little nudging on Esther's part, that I work up the nerve.

I tap him on the shoulder on the way out the door, and when he turns around I have it screen-up in my palm like a peace offering. "Can we talk?" It takes a second for it to register on his face, but once it does, his eyes move over mine. They're even darker than Mason's, but just as warm as he takes the phone from my hand.

We walk down the hall, away from Esther and the rest of the club coming out. Then, once we're far enough away that no one can hear us, I take the world's longest breath and come clean.

"I saw your password in class yesterday," I say. "Then I used it to look in your phone to read some of your texts with Vanessa."

Spencer's eyes grow wide, and those brown orbs that looked so warm a moment ago are now ice cold, bobbing like cubes between me and his phone. He doesn't ask why, but anguished lines form in his forehead as he exhales.

"I'm sorry," he says.

"You really cared about her, didn't you?" I think back to the funeral. How his grief angered me because I thought it was a fabricated lie, piggybacking on "real" pain, but all along he was hurting as bad as we were.

Spencer's lips quiver. Two tectonic plates sliding against one another until his whole body shakes next to me. If only she could see the aftershock she left in us all. He bites down on his bottom lip, nodding. "Yeah. I did. I wanted to tell you, I did. But—"

"I know. Cade didn't want you to tell me." He nods again, teetering on the brink of tears when I slip my arms around him in a hug. His arms eventually tighten around me, holding me as his sobs shudder both of us.

"I'm sorry," I whisper next to his ear.

I thought knowing for certain would mean a Band-Aid for my heart.

Like once I knew where she was going, the empty place carved in my chest would somehow fill back up and heal on its own. But mine wasn't the only heart full of questions just like Mason's wasn't the only one broken.

It's like we've passed that same sad breath around between her parents and me, to Mason, and now Spencer. Pulling out the pain, wearing it like one of her pins. Out in the open for everyone else to see. As if somehow, seeing it makes it less instead of more.

To: Bailey.Pierce@tchs.edu

From: Sawyerr_Bianca@stanford.edu

Subject: Stanford Application Interview

Dear Bailey,

I'm reaching out because we've reviewed your application for the 2022/2023 year. I'd like to set up an interview sometime next week to talk more about you and your goals for the future.

I'm looking forward to connecting and learning more about Alaska and your work with NewVision.

Please follow this link to schedule your interview. I'll email you back with a link for our video chat.

Sincerely,

Bianca Sawyerr

WHAT HAPPINESS FEELS LIKE

When Esther and I walk through the door, my moms are sitting at the kitchen table. Esther lets me hold it over their heads for exactly two minutes before she starts screaming about the email. Even though I tell them we already knew it was coming, Kat-Mom says progress is progress and demands we celebrate.

There are no Pop Rocks or champagne, but we order sushi and Esther stays over so we can play board games. My moms ask me to read and reread the email at least ten times so we can all squeal about it.

It's happiness. That little spark of excitement that begins with a smile watching Kat-Mom beam with pride. She says she can't wait to tell her parents, how they've been asking all week. How Jacky-Mom has already texted half her staff to brag about her kid. Me. She's bragging about me instead of bringing up the grades or saying I can do better.

Esther, my friend who has looked up the program in detail, is gushing about all the accolades and faculty at Stanford. And we dream about the things I'll learn while I'm there, and I profess that if I get in, we can make our very own *Saved by the Bell*–inspired Kevin robot when we come home for winter break. I'm not even sure that Stanford is something I want, or just something I'm supposed to want, but the energy is infectious.

I can't help but be excited.

When Cade texts, asking if he can come over and talk, I start to answer. But Kat-Mom has those eyes that beg me to set the phone down and enjoy the moment. I shoot him a quick message saying I can't tonight, but I'll text later.

Then set it aside, out of sight.

For the first time in months, the smile on my face isn't just reaching up into my eyes. It's strung around my heart, networking through my spine, down into every bone, digitized into my bloodstream.

And best of all, it's not a lie.

Bailey: Today was a big day.

I got an interview with Stanford!

V: what!?!?!?!?

that's amazing!

Bailey: It isn't a done deal, just an interview. But I'm excited.

That's not why I'm texting though.

V: is this about spencer again?

Bailey: Yeah.

I talked to him today.

V: about what?

Bailey: You.

V: shit.

bailey why?

why would you do that?

Bailey: I know you don't get it, but I had to.

I've spent months wondering where you went that night.

V: okay, bailey i need to tell you something.

Bailey: I already know.

Spencer wasn't just some guy for you.

V: bailey. please.

Bailey: It's all out now.

There's nothing left to say.

I just want you to know I'm happy.

It doesn't change how I feel about you. I still love you.

We can go back to our regularly scheduled banter and witty anecdotes.

Love you, you asshole. ☺

V: . . .

GOODBYE TO TONIGHT

A knock at the window pulls me from the conversation with V.

The sky has gone from gray to slate to midnight black.

Stars never sprinkle the atmosphere; there's no moonlight shining through the clouds.

When I hear the latch as Mason loosens the window, I hide my laptop between the nightstand and bed. Seeing him here in my room is almost like seeing him for the first time. Without any lens or filter, I'm face-to-face with exactly what this is.

The crease between his eyebrows is sadness.

Paint splotches on his shoes look like teardrops.

That duffel bag is his home.

And the girl he mourns, a liar.

The memory of her leaves him lonely.

We don't even speak. Not a word. But I scoot over to make room for him. His eyes are as black as the sky tonight, and when he lies next to me, I brush the hair out of his face and tears from his eyes.

No Bob Ross.

No trying to forget.

Just the sound of his heartbeat thundering over mine.

If he only knew how much he didn't know.

His eyes warm my body from the inside. Our eyes speak for us, expressing the indescribable combination of sadness and happiness. Grief and anger. The acknowledgment that if the imaginary line drawn between us in my bed was to dissolve—a blue flame turned red—we could never come back from it.

"Mason." I let his name sit between breaths. I have no idea what I meant to say because what comes out next rides on the vibration of something between fear and elation. "Can I kiss you?"

If I were one of those book girls, I'd have let out a breath I didn't know I was holding.

And Mason's right there, taking it in, like we're using the same sad breath to stay living. He reaches a hand up, tentative at first, grazing a finger along my cheek before he pulls me to him. Then in that space between anger and sadness and fear and everything else, we're kissing.

Heart-pulsing, explosive kissing that rips past every tear from these last months.

I-can't-take-this-back kissing I get lost in.

And I don't allow myself a single thought except that I have never wanted to be kissed as much as I do now. The kiss deepens, and instead of speaking with our eyes, we speak with our hands. His wander down my body, and mine tangle through his hair.

We break apart, staring for a long time, as if we're both trying to read out what the other is thinking.

Then, as if we're magnets instead of people, we kiss again.

RUIN

It's a perfect, blissful night of sleep.

The sounds of a phone chiming pull me awake. Last night flashes through my mind like lyrics to a song, snippets of verse that create a picture so clear my heart starts pounding all over again.

He shifts next to me, our limbs sliding against one another, until he's got his arm around me. Sleepily, he smiles, nuzzling up and kissing me right on the nose.

It's this sweet, simple little gesture that yanks me from the moment, reminding me that before last night—that perfect incandescent night—he was hers. I push away the voice in my head that says, *He's thinking of her still.*

The phone chimes again. Then again in rapid succession. Vibrating against the nightstand. Mason mumbles before reaching for the phone. "Is that you or me?"

He grabs it, opening his eyes, groggily handing it over to me.

Even though I'm squinting, the face recognition software does its thing, pulling up a preview for the texts I've received today. I shift uncomfortably when I see Cade's name there next to a string of messages from V the night before.

"It's Cade. He probably wants to talk."

I'm pushing back another thought. How it would feel for Cade knowing the dust hadn't settled on our breakup before I'd hooked up with my best friend's boyfriend. Ignoring the sickening lurch in my stomach, I hand my phone back, screen still lit with the message. "Can you plug it in?"

"Should I tell him you're busy?" A smile tugs at the corners of Mason's eyes as he holds my phone in his hand. Pretending to thumb out a message, he must accidentally exit the thread with Cade because when he looks down at the screen he asks, "Who is V?"

My heart stops.

No.

Panic spreads through me like wildfire. And I grab at my phone before he pulls it away, pressing something. His eyebrows come together in confusion as if he's trying to figure out what he's looking at. His jaw goes slack and I watch, helpless.

"Mason," I say, my voice quaking. "Please don't read that."

"What the hell?" He turns the screen to me, showing the steady stream of messages from V from last night. It's all there. His name. Mine. That she didn't mean to cheat on him. What's worse, as he's holding it, it doesn't stop chiming.

Ding.

Ding.

Ding.

Ding.

New ones from Cade dropping down as an alert at the top of the screen.

I reach again and Mason's face twists in disgust as he pulls away. "Please let me explain."

V: yes.

i cheated on mason.

bailey.

i'm so sorry.

i didn't want to hurt anyone.

you have to know that.

i didn't want to hurt mason.

and I didn't want to hurt you.

DONE

Mason throws the phone down to the ground like it's boiling through his skin. Bringing his hands up to his face, all he can do is shake his head, and my heart drops into my stomach as he pulls away from me.

"What is that?" His eyes are bulging in their sockets. I hold a finger to my mouth, motioning to the door. My parents are undoubtedly starting their morning, and while their bedroom is two floors up, the kitchen is not.

"It's this app I use. A bot I made with texts and emails and social media stuff. It's like . . . talking to Vanessa."

"Bailey—" Mason throws his hands between us, in that place where maybe Vanessa's been this whole time. His jaw tightens, and he grits his teeth as he asks, "How does it know all this?"

I hate myself.

I hate every stupid moment that brought me right here staring at Mason, having to say the words out loud. "I may have used . . . I may have stolen some texts to help create the bot."

"Wait." Recognition hitting his gaze like he's put together the same puzzle I have these last few months. "When you accidentally grabbed my phone. You didn't . . ."

We are incomplete combustion.

"I know. I messed up. I'm sorry. I didn't want you to get hurt." I stare down at my feet. Naked toes pressed to the floor like if I focus hard enough it'll keep me upright. "I just needed to know. You were fine not knowing, and no one else seemed worried about where she was going that night. I had—"

"—Bailey, I knew." He looks out the window, his lips tight. The same lips that kissed along my collarbone last night are now pressed into a tormented pout. Like one more word will send him over the edge. "I've known for months. I—"

"You knew about Spencer?" I sit on the edge of my bed, pulling from his disbelief. "Why didn't you tell me? Mason, you could have told me."

Why wouldn't anyone say something? Mason. Cade. Vanessa.

The crease in his brow softens, and Mason's head tilts like we're speaking completely different languages and he's having to translate. "Why would she be meeting Spencer?"

"Because that's who she was cheating with." I rewind the last three months in my head—starting with the funeral and right up to where Spencer confessed. "He's been working on the addition for Liz's house. He was there that night, and she was driving out to see him."

"Oh, Bailey, no. She wasn't meeting Spencer. Spencer just gave them the code," Mason says, falling on his knees in front of me on my bed. "I'm so sorry." His cheeks suck in, like his mind and mouth are fighting against one another. He's working through his thoughts, and every moment he isn't speaking is a moment my heart is gaining speed.

"Tell me." I'm shaking when his arms slide around me, holding me tight like he's preparing for me to fall apart—shatter, splinter like frozen puddles being stomped apart. I don't know how much time passes, but it feels like hours of agony. "You're scaring me."

Finally, he breaks. Voice raspy and unhinged. "It was Cade. She was meeting Cade. She was cheating with Cade."

THE CHILL

Last year, Vanessa talked me into raising money for some fundraiser so we could jump into a giant hole in an icy lake on New Year's Day.

The buildup was torture. Standing in a bikini, holding Vanessa's hand as we shook both from anticipation and the freezing temperatures. The plunge itself, ice-cold water covering my entire body and knowing there was absolutely nothing natural about the way it rattled my core. How the cold took the breath from my lungs and for a moment—as I pushed my way to the surface—I thought I might die.

We were scooped out, wrapped up in blankets. Vibrating, a hypothermic chill in our bones, as adrenaline moved us from the lake to a tent where we warmed up with hot cocoa and photos with our families. Our teeth chattered, and I told her I was sure I'd die. Vanessa just laughed and laughed before saying, "You asshole, that feeling is how you know you're alive."

That feeling right there, between dead and living. Hypothermic adrenaline—that's how it feels when Mason's mouth moves over the words.

She was cheating with Cade.

I'm back underwater. The chill seeping through my skin and landing in my soul. I'm looking at Mason, but I'm still underwater and his words land like a garbled, voiceless mess.

I stand, pulling away from his touch, and when he follows me toward the door I threaten to walk out of, I shove him in the chest—screaming. He's begging me to be quiet, but I can't. I'll never be able to scream as loud as it hurts.

When Jacky-Mom opens the door, eyes on me, on Mason, on the pile of bedding crumpled up at the end of my bed, I know I should care. I should feel guilt as Kat-Mom follows in behind her with her hand to her heart like my scream flipped her body inside out too.

But I'm too busy rewinding these months.

The wish she made on the pier—the tears.

Cade.

The apology texts from Spencer.

The clear and obvious picture in front of me and just how blind my grief was.

WEEK TEN

EXCUSED ABSENCE DAY ONE

My moms sit at the kitchen table across from me. Between us, my phone.

I come clean with every lie, starting with stealing the app from Jacky-Mom's computer. And Kat-Mom reaches for my hand when I struggle to tell them about stealing the phones and how Mason had been staying over for weeks on and off.

Jacky-Mom gets quiet, walking away from the table with my computer after Kat-Mom says she thinks it might be best if I don't use my phone for a few days. I need a break. It's good for all of us.

That night, I put Vanessa's jean jacket out with the trash.

Esther comes over with my homework.

We sit in silence for a long time, trudging through pages in our textbooks, because Esther is too nice to ask for details before I'm ready to give them. After we're done, and we go up to my room, I close the door and we sit on my bed and I unload all the details I can remember from Mason's confessional in front of my moms that night.

How the night of the accident, Cade got drunk and tried to fight Mason at Zoe's party. She broke it up, sent Cade home, but not before he implied that he and Vanessa had hooked up. Mason texted Vanessa, and went to her house, hoping to talk.

Only she never made it.

After she died, Liz's dad found a video from the doorbell camera on the house Spencer had been working on. Turns our Mr. Winters liked to keep a close eye on who comes in and out of the house during the remodel. The camera showed Spencer leaving work, then hours later his truck pulls up and he gets out of the car with Cade.

According to Mason, after the funeral, he and Liz started hanging out. Watching Mason fall apart is what prompted her to confirm what Cade said the night they met up at Liz's house. She even showed him the video. Apparently Cade was pretty drunk. The camera picked up the last moments of a conversation where he was going off on Vanessa. Loudly, and on speakerphone, he told her he couldn't keep doing this.

Mason said the last thing heard on the clip as Cade stumbled into the house was Vanessa's voice, asking where he was.

Esther listens in disbelief and tells me she's sorry as I clutch my stomach—remembering every detail after that night. Every time Cade and I kissed, how he wanted me to temper my grief. How every memory with Vanessa holds a different meaning now. How devastating it is to miss her and hate her with the same breath.

EXCUSED ABSENCE DAY THREE

On my third day out of school, I sleep in. A glorious, dreamless sleep that holds me like a hug. It's a patch of sunlight peeking through the fog, cast down through my window that might have woken me if Jacky-Mom hadn't done so first.

My moms were headed into Anchorage to run errands, but wanted to give me plenty of time to get ready for my interview in a few hours.

I walk downstairs, still in my pajamas from two days ago, to find a Post-it note from Kat-Mom, also reminding me about the interview. Letting me know, one last time, that it's totally fine to reschedule.

I sit in the living room, bingeing on crappy TV and eating an entire bag of cheese crackers. When the doorbell rings at midday, I wipe away the crumbs and trudge over, opening the door to see Cade standing on the other side.

He looks like he did at the funeral.

His face is wrecked. His cheeks are blotchy, and those impossibly blue eyes are rimmed red and swollen from crying. Running a hand through his hair, he searches me for something, and I force back a laugh as I realize he really is the screwed-up version of Prince Eric to Vanessa's very tragic Ariel.

Making a move for the door, I grip the handle, anticipating the rush I'll feel as I let it swing closed in his face. I don't see his hand flying up to stop it, and he takes a step forward and stands over me. "I'm sorry."

My throat burns with bile.

"You're sorry?" I rub my forehead like I can't believe I'm hearing this come out of his mouth. I can't help myself. "There's nothing you can say that will ever make me think you're anything but a monster."

He shrinks, mouth in a thin line as he looks away from me. I feel everything from the last few months bubbling like lava to the surface of a volcano. I'm so angry, my hands shake by my sides as I erupt.

"You want to talk? Talk." I move onto the porch, the door slamming closed behind me. He takes a step backward. "When?"

"While you were on your college trip." He practically vomits the words.

"Just once?" I ask, and this time it's absolutely a breath I know that I'm holding. When he doesn't respond, I go on. "So, you hooked up with my best friend. More than once. And then waited months to break up with me."

"I know." I hate how quiet he is. How he looks like a wounded bunny just taking everything I have.

"What were you doing with Spencer that night?"

"Bailey."

"Go on."

"Please."

"I'm waiting."

"He was at the party. After Mason and I got into it, he took me there so I could cool off . . . before I . . . did anything stupid. Bailey, you have no idea how much this has eaten me up."

"Great. You felt bad. What about *after* she died? How you gaslit me because I couldn't get past the fact that something wasn't adding up."

I watch him break, shatter right there in front of me, soul open. And as much as I want it to feel good that I finally get to scratch back at the surface of his scars, I can't. Because this was never what I wanted. No one is winning here.

"Why?" I ask. "Why couldn't you just leave me alone? Say hi at the funeral and go back to pretending I didn't exist. You didn't have to keep it going. Cade, you strung me along and made me think that I—"

"I loved her." His voice cracks through my tirade. The way he says it like it's got its own energy sends a sobering shock through me.

"So why start things back with me?" I ask, leaning against the frame of the door.

"Because being around you . . ." He kicks his shoe against the edge of the porch. "Being with someone who loved her too felt less lonely."

My heart sinks to my stomach, and the way Cade looks at me, head down, eyes up—like he's all out of excuses—I get it.

Because we've all been eating one another's grief. Cade holding me to forget the pain of Vanessa, while I was holding on to Mason.

INTERVIEW

I'm fine. I'm fine. I'm fine.

I log in on time, and I'm even dressed. The video chat with Mrs. Sawyerr starts up without a hitch. She looks exactly like I think an admissions director would look. Poised, with a pair of glasses that look a little like the ones Eugene Levy wears in *Schitt's Creek*, and she gets straight to the point as she asks all the questions I'd expect to be asked.

First up is what I think would make me a good candidate. Easy enough. I could answer that one in my sleep. I'm fine.

She sees I want to major in data analytics with a focus on machine learning. What does the future of machine learning look like to me? I'm fine.

I'm so busy holding it together I don't even realize I've wound my laptop cord into a tight coil around my index finger, but it all loosens when she asks, "How has machine learning and artificial intelligence impacted your life?"

"Oh, um. I guess in a lot of ways." I buy myself time with filler words, then start with the most obvious response. "Well, as you saw in my résumé, I worked with my mom at her company, NewVision, in the summer. They're responsible for a number of applications involving machine learning—"

I can hear the answer in my head. The words all in place and ready to be rattled out because this is what I do.

I'm fine. I'm fine. I'm fine.

Until I'm not.

"Sorry—" I say, realizing I've zoned out. "Right. NewVision."

Mrs. Sawyerr is looking directly into the screen and smiles in that encouraging way people do when you're about to completely flub something. I watch as she taps her pencil against her desk, then sets it to a pad of paper, writing something down. I could start back up—rattle out that very answer I was so sure about before—but I can't.

I'm not okay.

"I'm sorry—I have to be honest with you. Machine learning ruined my life."

Mrs. Sawyerr looks up; clearly I've gotten her attention. "Excuse me?"

"God, that felt so good to say." I exhale, slumping in my chair. "I reformatted an older app of my mom's this year. It was a good app by the time I got it the way I wanted it—the machine-learning element was incredible—and in a perfect world I'd be sitting here in this interview and telling you what an amazing opportunity it would be to attend Stanford. And don't get me wrong. It would be awesome, and my mom would be so damn—sorry. Sorry for swearing. But since

I started using that app, my entire world fell apart."

Her lips curve up in a smile, and she leans back in her chair as if she's watching a movie instead of interviewing a prospective student. "Would you care to elaborate, Bailey?"

"How much time do you have, Mrs. Sawyerr?"

REVISION

When my moms get home, we go through my computer and phone. They read the messages from Cade, deleting every one. They read me the ones that won't hurt, and help sort out the ones that will. Kat-Mom rubs my shoulders while I tell them about Cade showing up at the house, and they share one of those looks that let me know they probably watched the whole damn thing in the door camera.

And when Kat-Mom goes to make dinner, Jacky-Mom stays behind.

"I botched my interview," I say, noting the way her eyes narrow on me.

"Why do you think you botched it?"

"Oh, trust me." I heave out a breath. "It's botched."

Jacky-Mom fiddles with the sticker on her Hydro Flask, clearly mulling over something, and I can practically hear the disappointment humming from her like it's made with sonic energy.

"Mom, I'm really sorry."

She looks at me again, but this time there's something else there. She's not annoyed or frustrated; her expression is soft. "I went through your computer. And your phone." She tenses. "Full disclosure, I read through most of your conversations with the bot. I mean, it's pretty cool you were able to transfer them across platforms, but that aside, I want to talk to you about something I read."

I turn to her, eyes wide as I think back to everything V and I talked about. Every memory I disclosed, every confession.

"I'm not worried about that stuff." She waves her hand in front of her face, like it's nothing. Her red lips curl into a smile as she adds, "Though I'm considering that maybe you need a lock on your window."

I look down at my hands, my cheeks going red as I remember the way they found Mason and me in my room. The whole thing still feels like a nightmare.

"You said something in one of those texts with the bot," she says, and my heart races as she pauses to take a drink. "You said you felt pressure being my daughter."

I wince, wishing she'd found anything else, because I know what I screamed into the ocean that day.

She leans in, the thin lines around her eyes crinkling in the corners, brows raised. "I want to be clear. I'm proud of you. I love you. I love you no matter what you do. Whatever school you go to. Whatever program you follow. I'm sorry for pushing you so hard." Her shoulders shrug. "I thought I knew what you wanted. And I figured I knew how to get there, so I did what I could to help."

And then, after a lot of crying and apologizing from both of us, my mom wraps me up like she's one of those woodland fairies meant to keep me safe and says, "Promise me you'll only follow *your* dreams, and I'll promise to give you space to figure out what those are. Unless you feel like you're flying, it's not worth following."

TO FLY FREE

It's been years since I skied.

But when I wake up the next morning to snowcapped trees, it's all I want to do. To clear my head and feel like I'm flying. I find Kat-Mom's gear in the garage, and I bundle up extra before setting out for the trail. Luckily, living in Tundra Cove means I don't have to go farther than my backyard.

I'm terrible. Even worse than I was back when we were all on the team together. I fumble over my feet like Bambi during his first time on ice. I'm all feet, and I fall too many times to count, but every once in a while, I find a decent stride. Then I'm flying down the trails that Mr. Carson probably woke up way too early to carve.

The wind in my face bites like the winter cold it's born from. The snow falling makes it impossible not to stop and stare at the picturesque mountain caps all around me. I ski down the trail, passing people here and there who wave and say things like "Great snow, right?"

A wooden fence marks the trail's end and the crevasse below, and I slow at the approach, stepping out of the skis to walk along the edge. Vanessa would have hated this.

It looks still. Trees stemming from the ground, glazed with ice and dusted with powder. It's funny—when it snows, it makes everything seem fresh and new. Things look cleaner when everything beneath them is covered. But it isn't clean, not at all. Underneath it's just as messy.

It's so still, so quiet, I can hear my heart beating from inside every layer I wear.

On a perfect day, I can only think of the mess I've made, and how no amount of snow will ever be able to clean it. And in the end, no amount of snow could have cleaned up Vanessa's mess either. I grip the fence, calling out into the mountainside.

"I wish!"

My voice echoes, screaming back at me, "I wish, I wish, I wish" until it dies.

I hold my arms out and suck in the deepest breath.

"I wish I'd known!" I say, and repeat it again, only louder. "I wish she didn't cheat!"

But it's not enough. I pull in another breath and go again. "I wish I'd never touched that stupid app!"

I'm airing all my grievances now; back arched, I hang on the fence and scream my words until they echo even longer—coming back to me in a whisper, a hug. Finally, I pull in everything I have, and exhaust myself by screaming at the top of my lungs, "I wish

I'd never met Vanessa Carson!"

I catch myself on a sob, followed by another, and my third is interrupted by a voice attached to the sound of skis sliding to a stop on snow. I turn just as Liz pulls the hat off her head, shaking it free of snow. "Hey, welcome to the club."

THE AIRING OF GRIEVANCES

Liz slips out of her skis with the grace of someone who deserved to sweep every state title last year. Her boots crunch against snow, making their way right next to me at the edge of the fence. She looks over, and I stand there, embarrassment taking place of the release I felt moments ago.

"Don't let me stop you," she says, extending her arm toward the mountainside. "By all means, keep going."

"I—I—I didn't know anyone was—" The way I'm stumbling for something to say is almost as mortifying as the skiing I did on the way here.

"Yeah, I figured," she says coolly. "If it makes you feel any better, I kinda wish I hadn't met her either."

I don't know why it stings when she says it, but it does.

"It's different." I stare down, moving snow around with the tip of my boot.

"Oh yeah, for sure, you're the president of this club. Mason's likely got dibs on veep, but I get to be at least the treasurer." The way her chin tilts, a grim smile appearing on her lips, hits me somewhere in my chest.

It's the first time I've ever thought about how it might have felt from her perspective. How tearing down the Vail sign might have felt, how the thinly veiled short story Vanessa wrote for English sophomore year would have hit, the questions that lingered long after the rumor that Liz and Mr. Carson were involved was proven to be baseless. How that must have felt for her.

It was Vanessa's story, and up until right now, Liz was just a character in it.

"I'm sorry." I utter the tiniest apology.

"You know, my dad has this saying. He says if people have the capacity to be unkind to others, they have the capacity to be unkind to you." Liz stretches her arms over her head, leaning to one side. "I wasn't innocent. I'm too competitive, and I've done my fair share of shit talking. I definitely appreciated Mr. Carson telling her I was the better skier. But best I can tell, we were all just taking turns being shitty to each other. What's important is what you get out of it."

I scoff, huffing out a visible puff of breath. "What did I get out of this?"

"Well, for starters, it looks like you got a pretty kick-ass new friend. Esther and I have Gov together and she's cool as hell." Liz has a point. If it weren't for this whole nightmare of a year, I wouldn't have gotten to know Esther the way I have. "And Mason."

Just hearing his name sends a chill through my already freezing body. I wonder what he's doing right now. What he's thinking about.

"Pretty sure he's never going to speak to me again."

"You should talk to him." Liz cocks her head, winking at me. Clearly he told her what happened. "But when you do, can you make sure that you're, like, all in? Speaking as his friend, I have to say that if you hurt him, I'll mess you up. I don't know if you heard, but he's been through a lot this year."

"You know, I think I heard something about that." My smile matches hers, watching as she moves away from me toward her skis. "Thanks for stopping."

Liz turns around, brows raised. "Get clipped in. We've got a lot of catching up to do."

Bailey: Hey, it's been a while.

V: almost a week.

Bailey: So I need to say some things, and you can't interrupt me. Okay?

V: okay.

Bailey: Remember that time at the restaurant where you told the waitress that she should think of her friendship as a tree. Something about how the end of that friendship would mean growth for her.

That the leaves falling became mulch for the tree.

I think that's what I'm feeling right now.

Like this awful thing happened, but maybe it's going to help me grow?

Don't get me wrong. I will never understand what you did.

Or how you kept it from me.

V: bailey.

Bailey: No interruptions.

I trusted you with everything.

I loved you like a sister.

And you held my hand after we broke up.

You came over with your Pop Rocks and your ice cream and

357

you watched as I fell apart, and you knew it was because of something you did.

But the worst part about the whole thing is that I still love you.

When I think about it, I still feel like you're my sister.

The mess was always there, I just didn't know.

And now that I know, I wonder if maybe it would have been different if you could have been the one to tell me.

Maybe we could have gotten past it.

But we'll never get the chance because you aren't even real.

This image I've made up in my head of you sitting on the other end of these threads is fake because you died going to see Cade that night.

And I'm mad at you for cheating, yeah.

But I'm even more mad that you died because you didn't think you could tell me.

That's it I guess.

I just needed to say it.

V: i'm sorry.

i have nothing else to say.

i'm so sorry bailey.

Bailey: There's nothing left to say.

V: i know.

but bailey.

if i was real

if i wasn't dead i know what i'd say.

i wouldn't even have to draft it in my notes app.

Bailey: What's that?

V: you were one of my life's best parts.

i didn't deserve the friend you were to me.

Bailey: I'll miss you, you asshole.

V: miss you too, asshole ☺

ONE LAST GOODBYE

I pull out her laptop, smoothing my hands over the case before opening it. This time, when the password prompt flashes, I know exactly what will work.

ilovecade

The screen springs to life. The windows of her laptop feel strangely like her room, left exactly as they were the day she died. A warning that she hadn't backed up her computer in almost a year, her photo editing software in the corner, a book review website up in her browser.

As the messages start coming in, I press the mute button so I don't have to hear every single ding of the "I'm sorry" texts from Spencer. There must be hundreds.

Pulling up the Notes app, I'm not surprised to see they are sorted by topic. "books i've read," "bookstagram ideas," and "christmas wishlist" are at the top. I scroll through, laughing at some of them like, "places i want to have sex someday" and "list of rides i haven't been on at disney," but my stomach turns when I see the very last one.

"things i need to say to bailey"

things i need to say to bailey

if i were going to actually send this note i'd start with i'm sorry.

i have no idea how to tell you what i need to say. because how do you do that? how do you tell the person you love more than anything that you did something that will crush them?

the details aren't important, but maybe i need to write them down in case i ever have the courage to explain myself.

you were on that college trip with your moms, and mason went camping with his mom and sister because she was home for the summer. my dad and i got into this stupid fight about how much i'd spent on our amazon account. i went to the store to clear my head and get ice cream when i ran into cade. he convinced me to go to some party with him and all his hockey buddies. it wasn't anything. just a night out. we even sent you a picture. remember?

i drank, a lot. i know that's not an excuse, and it doesn't mean we aren't both responsible for our actions, but it's important to say. if i wasn't drunk it wouldn't have happened because no matter how i felt in that moment, i love you and i never wanted to hurt you. and i loved mason and didn't want to hurt him either.

i've thought a lot about the why. the truth is it wasn't thought out at all. at least not on my end. we were talking about dumb stuff, and i made a stupid joke, and then cade laughed. i kept going, and he kept laughing, and it was easy, right? light. not like conversations with mason where it always comes back to *something heavy or insightful. or even with you. i love you but you're intense sometimes.*

i knew it was wrong when i did it, but i had sex with him anyway because in that moment . . . i don't even know . . . it was thoughtless. that was the beauty of it. i wasn't thinking at all. it was that feeling when you fall into a book so hard you lose an entire day in the story. your world is lost for the one you're reading. the chapter we wrote that night killed the noise in my head. and it felt so good to not think about my dad yelling at me or college or disappointing anyone at all. being there for anyone at all. i was there for me only, and something about it felt like an author adding a bonus chapter that only i could read.

the next morning we agreed it couldn't happen again and we'd never speak of it. not to you. not to mason. not to each other.

but after that, every conversation i had with mason felt too heavy. like, i knew what it could be like, light and thoughtless, and it wasn't. so i broke up with mason. the way he cried will live with me until i die. it reminded me of hearing my mother cry whenever my dad cheated. left sobbing while he swept it away with an apology remodel. i wanted to be stronger than my dad, to break it off, because really, mason was better off without me.

but then he said he couldn't be alone. and i caved, because watching him hurt made me realize all those remodels were never about my mother or what she got from them. it was about how it absolved him. mason needed me.

and i was just empty. so we got back together and i never told you because i didn't want to have to lie to you about why.

i felt terrible, but i told myself someday it would be only a memory. when you got back i convinced you not to bring the guys to seward, and i wished we could stay friends until we died. you told me i was drunk, and we laughed about it, but really i was so messed up about what i did. and scared of losing you.

mostly i hated myself.

all summer it worked until school started and we were there together. the four of us. like old times, but it wasn't fine anymore. it was in these little looks he'd give me across the stairs while we were eating that would rip me back to what it felt like that night. the way he'd laugh at something i'd say in conversation that sent me spiraling back to my favorite story. at homecoming we were all dancing. i looked over at cade holding you. your eyes were closed, head on his chest, and you looked so quiet. and all i could think was that i wished it was me. it was later that night, listening to you talk about what you and cade were going to do for colleges and being devastated that his future was already written and i was just a bookmark between the pages i wanted so desperately to be written in.

and it was all so much worse because i knew he felt the same way. because after homecoming while mason was getting the car and you were in the bathroom, he told me he missed me. and it felt so good to know he reread that chapter in his head too. here. this moment right here unraveled something in my heart that i knew i'd never get back unless i had him.

cade did the right thing. he broke up with you, and i'm the worst person in the world, because when i went to your house with those pop rocks and tissues, all i could think about was the fact that he was single now. and later that week i was the one who showed up at his house, and i'm the one who whispered that i loved him, and i'm the one who kissed him just to get lost in those pages again. i initiated everything.

i was never better than my dad, but i wanted to be.

i almost told you so many times. but one look into your eyes that look at me like I'm the person who would never hurt you, and i know. without any doubt in my mind, you'd feel ten times as bad as mason did. you're my sister, and what i did to you was unthinkable. and it wouldn't be the same. mason may have needed me, but i need you. and the idea of losing you . . . i couldn't. i can't. it would be like never reading another word as long as i live.

so i've ended it. for real. because loving cade isn't worth losing you.

because i don't want to be the kind of person who repeats their mistakes so often they have to live in them. that they have to escape into other people's stories to forget the pain they caused. and every day when you pretend you don't notice cade pass our lockers, and mason's got his arm around me, i die a little. because there's no winner here.

i'm icarus, flown too close to the sun. this mistake i made, of feeling something with cade i can't take back. of knowing that if i were to give my heart what it wants it would break you. i'm sorry. with everything i have, my greatest regret will be what happened that night. that stupid, selfish moment that has dog-eared every page in our story and set the spine on fire.

WELCOME TO NEWVISION

App developer: Bailey Pierce

Version: 3.2

UPLOAD INFORMATION

DELETE

INTERACTIVE EXPERIENCE:

Jacqueline Pierce

V.

SETTINGS

ARE YOU SURE?

All information for this account will be lost.

FREEDOM

I.
HOVER.
OVER.
DELETE.

Standing at my computer, I think about how it'll feel to unload everything in the trash, like burning Cade's favorite jersey. I want it gone, but it feels a little bad too. Like maybe I NEED to burn it, but it's better for both of us if it isn't sitting in my closet for me to find in a few months.

Because we all know what happens when you remember the good times. They're just the lit end of a fuse burning toward bad memories and heartache.

I look to my right, where Vanessa's jean jacket has reappeared. It's folded neatly at the edge of my desk, with one of Kat-Mom's Post-it notes on top saying she wanted me to be sure before I really throw it away. I trace my fingers along the edge of the forget-me-not pin.

Mrs. Carson always insisted that forget-me-nots are an invasive weed. Something that needed to be pulled out, dealt with right away so it didn't invade her garden. But Vanessa always argued that it was a flower. She found beauty in the weeds.

She didn't care if it destroyed everything in its path. Beautiful is beautiful. And I guess this whole time I've been doing just that. Celebrating the beauty in the path of grief, living in memories because it was easier than seeing that it was eating me alive.

I pick up the jacket, walking it over to my closet, and give it one more hug before I put it away. I'm not that girl stuck in the weeds. Not anymore.

Bailey: Hey I got my phone back.

And I want to start by saying that if you aren't ready to talk yet, I completely understand.

I did sorta commit a felony and all by stealing your phone.

But I'm sorry.

And as for the bot. I deleted the whole thing.

I'm ready to talk when you are.

Mason: tonight ok?

Bailey: I'll ask my moms.

Mason: Wait are we going legit? Front door and everything?

Bailey: Pretty sure my moms will kill you if you don't.

MASON, MY MASON

I see him on the screen of the doorbell monitor and tell him I'll be down in a second.

My moms beat me to it, and by the time I clear the stairs, they've opened the door—playing this fun game where they pretend like it's the first time they've met him as anyone but Vanessa's boyfriend, glazing over the awkward encounter from before.

Behind him, the sun shines brightly for the first time all winter. He's wearing a new hoodie, free of any paint on the sleeves, but I can tell by the way he holds his hands in the front pocket that he's got something hidden there.

Kat-Mom makes some excuse about how they need to do something in the kitchen, and Jacky-Mom takes a second to catch on. As they disappear, Mason kicks off his shoes, following me into the living room.

We sit down on the couch, and it's strange, seeing him after everything.

"Hey," he says.

"Hey back." I point to his pocket. "What's in there?"

"Oh, this?" Mason pulls his hands out of his pocket, turning his phone for dramatic effect. Wagging his eyebrows before setting it down. "I thought you were done with your thieving ways."

I grab the nearest throw pillow and hit him with it. And I call him a jerk, but I'm thankful that the tension between us has dissipated.

Mason reaches back in the hoodie pocket and pulls out a few packs of Pop Rocks. "I figured we might need these. Heavy conversation impending and all."

I stare into his deep brown eyes, thinking about every minute we've gone through these last few months. How daunting this has been. How neither of us has been able to get a moment's rest since that night. Maybe longer.

"Nah." I snap the plastic bags out of his hands before he has time to question it and toss them on top of the pile of mail on the end table. "No heavy conversation."

"No?" he asks.

"Let's skip the Pop Rocks. I'd rather just hang out. A couple of people sitting down outside of the Pop Rocks and Bob Ross and just . . . getting to know each other?"

His entire face goes blank at first, but he nods, easing a little closer to me too. And we aren't two people living off the same sad heartbeat anymore. But two people letting their hearts beat side by side.

Bailey: ANSWER YOUR PHONE!

What are you doing right now?

Esther: Would you believe something cool like sitting at a party, smoking weeds and drinking boozes?

Bailey: On a Sunday morning?

Not a chance.

But you're already cool.

You don't need to smoke weeds or drink boozes.

So I checked the application portal for Stanford a little bit ago…

Esther: And?!

Was it updated?????

Bailey: I guess I didn't bomb that interview as much as I thought.

I GOT ACCEPTED!

Esther: WHAT?!

Bailey, this is amazing! I'm so happy for you! You're gonna rock the cardinal colors this fall.

Bailey: Yeah, I'd totally rock them…

If I was going.

Esther: Wait what?

Bailey: It was funny. I was sitting there, staring at the acceptance, and I couldn't feel it. You know? Like yeah, cool I got in to Stanford. But also, I realized I was kind of hoping for a rejection.

Esther: Oh Bailey.

Bailey: But my moms obviously saw I wasn't feeling it and we talked.

So after a LONG conversation where Jacky-Mom almost pulled her hair out at the thought, I'm going to apply for a deferral and take a gap year! Maybe hang out here with you until I figure out what I want.

Esther: OMG!!!!!

Seriously?!

Bailey: And since you're going to school nearby . . .

Esther: We can hang out!!!

Bailey: Exactly.

Esther: I love this idea!

Bailey: I'll still be working at NewVision.

I figure at the very least I'll learn something. It's an opportunity to get to know who I am without Vanessa. And who knows—maybe I'll go to Stanford someday and do all the machine-learning stuff. But I'm kind of looking forward to putting it all away for a while.

Esther: I love this journey for you!

Seriously, Bailey.

You're brilliant. You'll be great at whatever you choose to do.

Bailey: Thank you.

You're a good friend, Esther.

Which leads me to my next question.

What are you doing tonight?

My moms are making pizza to celebrate my non-college going, and Mason is coming over to play games.

You in?

Esther: Yeah, for sure!

WEEK EIGHTEEN

Esther: Want to hear something super fun and awesome?

Bailey: Literally always.

Esther: I just edited the pictures from prom! Go check your email! I sent you the link!

Bailey: Ahhhhhh omg you and Spencer look so good!

Esther: Thank you! I'm glad I went with him. He was really nice.

Bailey: And Liz's tux is hot.

Like, I could never pull it off.

But she makes it look good.

Esther: I KNOW.

Did you see the pic I took of you and Mason dancing?

Bailey: Yeah ☺

Esther: Pretty cute.

Bailey: Yeah ☺ ☺ ☺

Esther: What are you doing right now? Want to come with me to print some off?

Bailey: Actually, I can't.

Mason should be here any minute.

We're meeting Vanessa's parents for the burial this afternoon.

Esther: Oh my gosh Bailey!

Why didn't you tell me?!

I'm so sorry. Here I am going on about prom pictures and you're doing this big heavy thing!

Bailey: You know what?

I think I'm actually okay.

Don't get me wrong, this is complicated.

Like, I knew that they'd bury her someday when the ground finally thawed.

Four months ago I thought it would feel like an eternity.

Esther: It's gone by pretty fast, hasn't it?

Bailey: It has.

But you know what?

I think it's better this way.

Last time I said goodbye to the Vanessa I thought I knew.

And this time I get to really say goodbye.

Esther: That's a beautiful way to think about it.

You go.

We'll print pictures later.

Bailey: Can't wait.

FORGET ME NEVER

We're a few minutes late leaving for the burial because Kat-Mom wouldn't stop talking to Mason about the painting he presented for the end-of-the-year artist showcase. A beautiful, serene mountainside scene, covered in snow.

An image I recognized as soon as I saw the initial sketches. A winter scene with a stillness to it that makes it look as if it's holding its breath. The same snowy mountain Mason and I looked out over that day we almost slid into the moose.

He called it *Vanessa's Song*.

On the way to the burial site, Mason is silent. He's not wearing his typical hoodie but a button-up shirt and tie. The same ones he wore to the funeral, and something about seeing him wear them makes it feel like we've time traveled. Last weekend at prom we were above the water of grief, maybe even out of it. Sitting on the beach, enjoying the sun.

Today it feels like we've been pulled back beneath the waves.

"You know," I say to Mason as we hit the edge of Tundra Cove, slipping onto the highway. "It doesn't really feel like she's gone."

"I know." He adjusts the rearview mirror, looking back. "But at the same time . . ."

"It feels like she's *really* gone." I look to the mountains as I finish his sentence.

Everything has changed since she died. Even the way the world looks.

Evergreen trees dot a path up to Raven Pass. Bright green leaves line the birch trees dispersed between them, and the entire road is well lit, bathed in sunlight. Snow is but a memory to the flowers that have bloomed all around the wooden cross still standing in the spot that marks her death. I know because I was there just a few days ago.

"Well, you know there's the old cliché, right? How the people you love never die because they live in your memory." Mason's eyes move over mine before they go back to the road.

He's not wrong.

This year was supposed to be filled with memories. Choosing colleges landed a little different for me, and for Vanessa's parents, of course, who had to field acceptance letters from three different schools. How proud they were. Decision Day, where I imagined which of those colleges she would have chosen, which was obvious. Florida State all the way.

Vanessa was even there on our senior trip when Esther and I went

382

to Seattle for a weekend. I made sure we stopped by her favorite independent bookstore, and wouldn't you know, the author of *Forget Me Always* was doing a book signing. It was kismet.

And prom. It was magical. That sweet picture Esther took captured the literal moment Mason and I danced under the streamers and lights, talking about how much Vanessa would have loved it.

She'll be at graduation too, with a whole slideshow devoted to her memory.

"It's funny. I spent a lot of time worrying about the pieces of her that live in phones and computers or online," I say, "but I forgot that part of her still lives in all of us. Parts we do get to keep just for us."

"The best parts," he says. "The best memories."

Vanessa saw those lights and streamers at prom through me. Through Mason. And she danced around the house on Decision Day with her Seminoles sweatshirt because I imagined it. In Seattle, she got that book signed after waiting an hour in line—picking up the daisy-shaped enamel pin with it—because I did. Every moment, she got to live through me, because she's still part of me.

Mason pulls into the parking lot next to the graveyard. I try not to look at him as I reach into the back of his semi-cleaned-out car to grab Vanessa's jean jacket. It's so much a part of her, it deserves to be there. Tears form at the corners of my eyes, and even though I thought I was ready for this, I'm not so sure anymore.

"Hold on." Mason stops me, bringing a hand to mine, and squeezing it. "I thought today might be a hard day."

"I'm fine," I lie. "Come on, we need to go."

"Someone once told me that there's a pretty quick remedy for bad days," Even though his skin is warm, a chill runs through me. He smiles a soft sort of smile, reaching into the center console of his car and pulling out two plastic bags. Pop Rocks. Blue Raspberry. "I thought you might need these."

BURIAL

By the time we get out to Vanessa's gravesite, Mr. and Mrs. Carson are already there with one of the priests from Saint Christopher's.

They're hand in hand, holding on to one another as Mason and I approach the forget-me-not-covered casket. It's hovering over the burial plot, where Vanessa will lie forever. I try not to think about what it looks like inside the casket as we greet them.

"I'm so, so glad you both could come." Mrs. Carson hugs me tight, whispering at my shoulder. "I'd hoped you'd wear the jacket."

Her hair is cut in a short pixie cut, an entirely new version of herself, but she seems just as fragile as she was at the funeral. Even still, she musters a smile that never meets her eyes. Jacky-Mom once told me that when she had me it was like watching part of her heart sprout legs and walk away. That when I fell, she could feel her stomach drop. When I cried, she got the sting of my tears behind *her* eyes. I guess when your child dies, part of you dies too.

After she lets go, she reaches for Mason while Mr. Carson stands awkwardly at her side. I step forward, extending my arms to offer a hug that he accepts. Because even if the tiniest part of Vanessa is living in me, I'd know she'd want to hug her father.

When I pull away, he's smiling a teary smile, pointing to his lips before asking, "Blue Raspberry?"

"Oh crap, I forgot." I cover my mouth as Mr. Carson laughs a little.

"I was going to ask," Mrs. Carson says, having let go of Mason. "Don't feel bad, honey. You know Vanessa wouldn't have wanted it any other way. We've got about ten packs in the car."

She's absolutely right. If Vanessa could have chosen her own burial, there for sure would have been Pop Rocks. And I'm so thankful Mason thought of them too, because now that the ice is broken, it feels bearable. Less scary.

Like maybe we've found a life jacket in those Pop Rocks.

The priest steps forward, clearing his throat while looking at his watch. His voice is gentle when he asks, "Is this everyone?"

We all look at each other.

Mr. and Mrs. Carson, the complicated, bookish parents who should have never had to say goodbye to their only daughter.

Mason, the artistic and broken-hearted boyfriend who always had a grand romantic gesture up his sleeve.

And me. The comedic-relief best friend every bookish girl needs.

"No," I say. "We're still waiting for—"

"I'm here!" Cade steps in with the rest of us, cheeks red, chest heaving like he ran all the way from where he parked. His impossibly blue eyes look anywhere but at the casket. "Sorry. My truck died and I had to borrow my dad's."

Cade. The one who should have made the obituary outtakes, but did not. Her secret. Her wish. The boy she loved.

WHAT SHE'D WANT

When we're walking back to our cars, Mr. and Mrs. Carson start asking Mason about his college plans. He's telling them all about Cornish and what scholarships he earned, while Cade and I linger behind.

He shuffles his feet against the grass, head down.

It's not like we haven't talked outside class. A few weeks ago, I ran into him and his dad at the grocery store. Then I told him congrats on Decision Day when I saw he was wearing a University of Denver hockey sweatshirt. And last week, after a very awkward conversation with Vanessa's parents, I texted him to see if he wanted to be a part of today.

He should be here.

This is, however, the first time we've been even sort of alone since that day on my porch.

"How are you?" I ask.

"Me?" Cade looks up from the ground, and the same eyes I used to get lost in find me. "I'm okay. You?"

"I'm okay." We stop, facing one another, while Mason and Vanessa's parents continue on without us. Cade can tell me all he wants that he's okay, but he forgets I know what his lying face looks like. The downturned smile, the uncomfortable shift in his shoulders. "Cade. Really. How are you?"

"I don't know." He pushes his hands down into his pockets, shrugging. "I was having a pretty hard time there for a while. When you found out, I felt like . . . I don't know. I felt like you hated me."

"To be fair," I say through a half-grin, "I did call you a monster."

"To be fair," he half grins back, "I deserved it."

After a beat, the smile fades and he says, "I'm sorry. For everything. Even after she was gone. I really messed everything up."

"Me too. Which reminds me. I have something for you." I reach up, finding the forget-me-not pin over my heart. I release the pin, slipping the back out of the pocket before replacing it. Pinching it between my fingers, I reach for his hand and place it right in the middle of his palm.

The way he looks at it, like he's trying to keep himself from crying, turns my stomach on itself. I almost regret the gesture before he asks, "Are you sure?"

"I think, of all people, she'd want it with you," I say, using my hands to force Cade's hand closed around it. Then, before we can say any more on the subject, I loop my arm through his, and take a step toward the parking lot where Mason is still talking to the Carsons.

As we get closer, Cade nods toward him. "So you and Torres, huh?"

"Hey, you weren't the only one afraid to be alone with your grief." I swat at his arm, and he winces, pretends it hurt. I turn, looking up at him. "Is it weird?"

"Nah," he says, looking down at me. "Maybe at first. But I think, in the whole backward way all this went down, it's pretty cool you have each other. I don't think she'd want—"

He starts to say something else, but stops, swallowing his words.

"I don't think she'd want any of us to feel bad forever." I stop again, grabbing his shoulders to look at him. Really look at him.

He's not a monster at all, but a boy living under the weight of his mistakes.

I think about what Liz said that day on the mountain. How we were all just walking around taking turns being shitty to each other. Me, Mason, Vanessa, Liz, Cade. None of us should have had to carry this much pain. Not ever.

"You deserve good things too, Cade." I wrap my arms around him, hugging him, because the last thing Vanessa would have wanted was for anyone to hurt this long.

Bailey: It's weird texting your actual phone now, but here goes. We buried you today. It was ten times better than your funeral, by the way. But also ten times harder. Anyway, I've been thinking about what V said before I deleted her. How if she was real, she knew what you'd say. That I was one of your life's best parts. Now, what happened was awful. Seriously. Wouldn't wish it on my worst nemesis. And there was a brief period of time where I thought maybe you were my actual nemesis. But I'm sitting here in my living room watching Mason laugh at Jacky-Mom's De Niro impression and Kat-Mom tell Esther how to grow an herb garden in winter. We've been playing Phase 10 for hours. And it occurred to me that I'm happy. Really happy. In a way that I didn't think was even possible after you died. So I just wanted to let you know that even after everything, you were one of my life's best parts too. I hope wherever you are, there are Disney Princesses. And Pop Rocks. And enough books that you never have to read the same page twice. I hope you write the next great heavenly novel. And that you get to go to prom with some really hot angel or something. But mostly, I hope you're happy too. Really happy. Like we all deserve to be. I love you, you asshole. **Error:** MESSAGE NOT FOUND.

Acknowledgments

I'd like to start by saying that this year has been the hardest of my life, and I have a lot of people to thank for getting me through it. So buckle up, because this is about to be a long list of acknowledgments and "I love you" proclamations.

First, to my readers: thank you. Thank you for being part of this journey with me, because without you I wouldn't be able to write stories. And for sharing your stories with me. Every message I get saying how you connected with my book is fuel to keep going. Thank you for being vulnerable with me and allowing me to be vulnerable with you too.

To The Bent Agency family: Louise Fury—thank you for being such a great agent. Not only selling books but remaining a sounding board who always does their best to put good things in the world and help others do the same. You inspire me. Jenny, Nicola, Victoria, Gemma, Claire, Nissa, Molly, Sarah, James, Martha, Zoë, John, Laurel, and Desiree—thank you for being part of the power team, and for all the collaborative efforts you bring and put behind every story that passes through TBA! Your support is invaluable. Amelia Hodgson, thanks for all that you do. Also, Sean Berard at Grandview LA—thank you for everything you've done for my story as well.

To the Quill Tree family: Alyssa Miele—thank you for sending Pop Rocks, offering incredible feedback, and mostly for believing in me and this book (even when I didn't think I could do it). You never doubted me for a second! I'm so grateful for you. Rosemary Brosnan—thank you for putting such an amazing team together. I am so proud to be part of it. Jon Howard and Robin Roy and Jessica

White—thank you for everything you did to make sure this story was polished. Sorry about all the texts and intentional errors—this book had to be a copy editor's nightmare! To the design team: David Curtis—you truly brought this story to life on the page. Those chapter headers!!!! And Jack Hughes, for the cover art—seeing Cordelia for the first time as art is something I'll never forget. Thank you. Shannon Cox, Lena Reilly, and the rest of the marketing team—you are truly incredible. Thank you so much for everything you all do.

To a few of the creators who inspire me: Meg Cabot—*The Boy Next Door* was the first book I read as an adult that felt different. The structure, while I didn't even realize it, was influencing me to take those chances all these years later. Lin Manuel Miranda—reading *Hamilton: The Revolution* gave me the inspiration I needed to play with structure and step outside of the "norm," to try something new. Taylor Swift—*Folklore* and *Evermore* fueled me during this pandemic and watching you try new things not only invigorated me but inspired me.

To my friends, my confidants, my sisters in life: Amy Wamy—thank you for always being there for me. Knowing that I have you on speed dial, offering to leave on the next flight out just to hand-feed me Pop Rocks means everything to me. I love you. Rajessica—thanks for being there to talk, always. I love you. Kiki—you're not here to see the mess but always there to pick up the pieces with a call. I love you. Nicole Brown, Elizabeth Burke, Moira Gallagher, Lisa Brandsetter, Chloe Laughlin, Tara Harmon, Sylvia Salazar, Katie Liestman, Trista Wilson, Veronica Pope, Lindsay Belle Sobalik, Jen Baker, Suzie Smith, Sarah Sundberg, Sarah Freije, Adrean Czajkowski, Enjoli Strait, Audra

York, JoAnn Latham, Brenna Butcher, Ciji Porter, Scott Morrison, Nicole Wilkins—thank you for being there for me at a point in my life when I needed you. Even if it was years ago, I needed you then, and you were there, so you're a friend in my heart to this day.

To my community: Alaska Writers Guild, SCBWI Alaska, and the faculty at APU—your support has been incredible, and I'm grateful to be a part of this community. Brooke Hartman, Dave Onofrychuk, Jamey Bradbury, Don Reardon, Marc Cameron, Stefanie Tatalias, Jena Benton Lasley, Matt Lasley, Jeremy Pataky—thank you for everything you do for Alaska and the writers who live here.

To my writing communities: The entire Pitch Wars family—thank you for pushing me and inspiring me to help others in their journeys: Brenda Drake, Ayana Gray, Gail D. Villanueva, Sarah Nicolas, Kellye Garrett, Sonia Hartl, Irene Reed, Leigh Mar, Rebecca Mix, Laura Lashley, Roselle Lim, Luke Hupton, Rajani Larocca, Susan Lee, Juliana Brandt, Remy Lai, Bethany Mangle, J. Elle, Emily Thiede, and Michael Mammay: thank you for everything you do. It has been such an honor to be part of such an amazing mentorship program. My Clubhouse family: Jennifer Bailey, Sona Charaipotra, Naz Kutub, Hannah Sawyerr, AJ Oakes, Alex Harper, Andy Leo, Leira Lewis, Taj McCoy, Rachel Strolle, Racquel Henry, Ariel Vanece, Melody Simpson, Olivia Liu, Harper Glenn, Ines Lozano, Kristin Dwyer, Marlayna James, Ronni Davis, Meg Watt (+Jess Ekker, Shay Tibbs, and all the bees), Hyunjin, Lily Santiago, Glenn Farrington, Peter Kaufman, Jordan Barnes, Alainna MacPherson, Fatima Fayez, Erika James, Savannah Gardiner, Samantha Jon, and anyone else I've missed—thank you so much for all your insight, support, and love! And to the rest of the writing/book community in my life, most notably: Jessica Kelly, Nita Tyndall, Clelia Gore, Rey Noble, Erica Waters, Faith Gardner, Brittany Kelly, Joy McCullough, Ellen Hopkins, Rachael Lippincott, Suzanne Park, Britt Siess, Mike Lasagna, Cody Roecker, Rebecca Hanover, Emily Vajda, Nora Shalaway Carpenter, Rocky Callen, Alex Richards, Kyrie McCauley, Kathleen Glasgow, Jenna Evans Welch—thank you for being part of this journey with me. And of course, Jeff Bishop—without your encouragement and support I would be lost (was that worth a five-star rating on TikTok?) Ally Malinenko, Vianna Goodwin, and Margot Wood—you have no idea how much your support has meant to me this last year. You shared your grief alongside mine and I will never forget that kindness. Thank you. I love you all.

A huge, HUGE thanks to the #Bookstagram and #Booktok communities—you are truly incredible and have been pivotal in getting the word out there about this book! Your love of books is why writers like me get to keep telling stories—thank you so much for everything you do.

And to my closest writing partners: Deborah—who knew it would come to this? I can't believe how much we have lost and gained while writing stories alongside each other. Through it all, we still have each other, and we still have story. I love you. Vanessa—watching you debut this year has been an inspiration. The support you've given me through everything is invaluable, and I'm proud to call you my friend. I love you. Lindsay—I will never be able to thank you enough. Growing up with you side by side as authors will always be an honor. I love you. Mikki—my soul sister. Thank you for always listening and finding my keys (and talking through books and life with me) from a million miles away. I love you. Liz—my co-mentor, my favorite nemesis, my partner in fun. Thank you for being so supportive in this last year. I love you. Jennifer—the Rory to my Lorelai. You are by far my favorite pandemic surprise. I can't thank you enough for the countless phone calls, the late-night rehashes of TV shows, and, most important, the book-writing help! I love you.

To my extended family: Auntie Di, Uncle Frank, Grandma and Grandpa Walter, my husband's family in Wrangell, my family in Louisiana (with far too many to name)—thank you for your support. I love you.

To my home: Talon, thank you for holding me while I sobbed through that last draft. Knowing I have you beside me has made this year doable. You will always be my constant, my support, my love. I love you. My beautiful children—thank you for all your patience and cheerleading. You are the reason I follow my dreams, and I promise to help you follow yours one day too. I love you more than anything or anyone.

To my sisters: You are my sounding boards first and foremost, and the women I look up to and lean on. Without you, my stories wouldn't have a heartbeat. Beth—my first baby, my first sister, my forever friend. Thank you for being the constant in my life that you are. I can't wait to read your book someday. I love you. Crystal—thank you for teaching me how to love aside loss, and to never let it pull from the experience of growing. I'm so proud of who you are, and I know your mom and dads are looking down on you so, so proudly too. I love you. Bobo—thank you for seeing me. It's hard to ever imagine a world where our love for one another wasn't the bond that we have today. I'm so lucky to have your support. I love you. Danae—you have taught me so much this year—and have we been through it or what? Thank you for always being there. I'm so lucky to have you in my life and to raise children with. I love you.

To my moms: Mom #1—thanks for giving birth to me. Without you, I wouldn't be here writing books and following my dreams. Thank you for reading to me and taking time to bring me to the library all the time, and for never saying no to getting me more books. I love you. Dianne, my Bonus Mom—thank you for loving me and my sisters, being a grandma to our babies, and never for a moment making it feel like we aren't yours. And for every smile you put on Dad's face. His last years were so filled with joy, and that was in no small part due to the fact that you loved him so fiercely. I love you.

To my other set of parents: Dawn and Max—I can't even begin to tell you how much you mean to me. Dawn—you have taught me so much about family and love and what it means to protect that. You help keep my life (and the kids') in order, always have a space for me at the house, and never make me feel like I'm "just" your daughter-in-law. I love you. Max—thank you for all your book suggestions. I'm holding on to them for the right project. ☺ And thank you for all the spam, pranks, and encouragement you give me. In all seriousness, you always show interest and let me talk about this journey, and I appreciate it so much. I love you.

To Dad: it's a little weird to write an acknowledgment for someone who isn't here anymore, but here we are. The fear of losing you fueled so much of this story. I wish you could be here so I could share this journey with you, but the fact that your legacy lives in my heart forever has to be enough. Thank you for always being vulnerable with me, and for leaving the legacy of love to me, my sisters, and your bride. We have each other in the wake of losing you, and for that I am grateful. I love you.